DOWN RIVER

A STROLL
THROUGH THE SEASONS
AND COMMUNITIES
OF THE MIRAMICHI

Nonie Creaghan

Gaelóg Press

Down River

Featuring original Illustrations by Edith Pieperhoff on signature pages and adapted for end of chapter vignettes

Other vignette illustrations variously sourced and modified for this publication

Book design by Helena Mulkerns

CONTENTS

INTRODUCTION

The Miramichi River winds its way through a beautiful valley, has many little branches, and flows into a bay of the same name. Small farms were at one time scattered up and down the Miramichi River and around the bay, and fishing was a major occupation of the people.

Some say the name signifies 'land of plenty'. Others say it is called 'land of the strange people'. Some even call it 'land of the bad people'. Whatever it means, there is a unique mix of Mi'kmaq, Acadian, English, Scottish and Irish communities living together on the banks of the river. Other cultures have now joined in to create a rich blend of people in the northeast area of New Brunswick.

Before Europeans set foot on Canadian soil, Canada was inhabited by native peoples. For many years after foreign settlement on their lands, their struggle for survival was great. Today the Native Americans of Canada are restoring their culture and dignity, which was jeopardized in the birth of a new nation. There are several first nation communities in the Miramichi area on the east coast of Canada.

The Acadians played an important part in the early history of New Brunswick, Canada, and continue to do so. They had an enormous influence on art, crafts, language and music. The Acadians had a thorough knowledge of the land, and how to survive in it. They used local resources and developed a unique cuisine.

The stories in Down River were collected in the 1950s and 60s by Nonie Creaghan, whose family had lived in the area for generations. Her daughter, the author and poet Sandra Bunting originally wrote the poem that opens the book, "Who has heard of my Province?", and wanted to make it available as a book to be enjoyed by children and adults of Miramichi and further afield.

Life on the river has changed since these stories were written but the flavour of the land remains the same.

WHO HAS HEARD OF MY PROVINCE?

by Sandra Bunting, 1967

Who has heard of my province?
Is it forgotten or unknown?
I come from a land of rivers
that for a century has not grown.

Who has heard of my river?
For salmon fishing she's named.
Many subtract from her rich streams
and enter woods in search of game.

In your cities royalty is a memory
in the names of well-laid streets.
Queen Elizabeth imports fiddleheads
and New Brunswick sugar beets.

Rich farm land along the banks,
the cause of quiet market towns,
not changed much since first settled,
except for their modern sounds.

Forests almost destroyed by fire
shelter the deer and moose,
clumps of perfumed violets near a woodland path
shaded by dense forests of spruce.

In autumn, harvest time comes,
roads lined with maple leaf,
make up a colourful quilt,
beauty in ruggedness, not a coral reef.

The sun is hot in the summer,
the winter piled high with snow.
Oh, with all your beauty
why did I have to go?

Your main export is people.
You know why they go away;
industry's scarce, so with sisters
in Alberta or Ontario they stay.

With the beauty of your seasons,
why can't you hold their minds?
Don't ever change, be yourself
for only true people your beauty finds.

Meriku of Mi'kmaq Village

The Wonder Fish

Meriku waved at the big white boat until it grew smaller and went out of sight. Her daddy would drift in the boat in Miramichi Bay overnight to fish. Meriku walked along the rocky shore. As she walked, she collected pretty stones, a starfish and shells. She hid her treasures in a small cave, and sat digging her bare feet into the sand.

The sound of voices and barking dogs made Meriku run. She ran until she reached "the point," and then walked around the shore to the river on the other side. In the middle of the river, on the other side, was a grassy little island. Meriku wanted to cross over to the island, but she couldn't swim, and no one would take her. She picked up a piece of red coloured glass on the shore. She examined it, and looked through it with one of her big, round, brown eyes.

The grassy island sparkled through the glass. It was beautiful! Meriku threw the glass back on the sand, and as she did, she saw a flat round stone. She picked it up and clutched it gently in her fist. A sand dollar! Meriku rubbed the stone on her face. She looked over to the little island and saw a strange, shiny big silvery boat coming towards her at great speed. Her eyes opened as wide as they could. Before Meriku could even move, the great big silvery thing was ashore. It was the biggest salmon she had ever seen!

Meriku looked at the sand dollar, then looked at the salmon. Her face broke into a big smile.

"Where did you come from?" she asked.

"From the deep waters of the bay," the fish answered.

Meriku put out her hand and patted the fish gently.

"Climb aboard," the fish commanded.

I can't swim. And you're slippery," Meriku answered

"Climb aboard," the fish said again.

Meriku climbed on the salmon's back. It wasn't slippery after all. It was as if something held her down. The salmon skimmed over the river, and around the point. They rode the waves on Miramichi Bay, and the waves splashed over them. It was such fun that Meriku didn't even mind being wet! The big salmon turned and headed back to the river. He brought Meriku up to the little grassy island.

The island shore was light golden sand, and it felt like velvet under the little girl's feet. Meriku licked the salt from her lips as she walked. The salmon waited as the little girl explored. Meriku walked around and across the island. The sun was going down when she returned to the salmon. "It's time to go", the fish said. Meriku climbed on his back, and within a few minutes she was back on the village shore.

Digging for Clams

Meriku laughed. She laughed because it was the kind of day that tickled her humour. The sun shone brightly over the Mi'kmaq village. The air was warm and the wind teased the sea grass on the shore. She walked around the point with a pail in hand. People from the Beach Village had been around looking for clams to buy and she was going to dig some.

The best clam beach was around a bend on an inland river that flowed out to Miramichi Bay. Meriku decided that the river must be a refuge and resting place for fish because it was always so quiet and calm, lacking the force of the bay water.

She wondered if it was salty. She bent down and scooped up a fistful of water between her hands. She tasted it. Though salty, it was different from bay water.

She discovered a stretch of beach marked with small holes. Clams usually made their home beneath them. She knelt and dug with her two hands until she reached a clam. She put it in her pail and began digging again. Soon the pail was half full.

It was hard work and she was tired so she put the pail aside for a moment and rested. She looked out at the water and there at the edge was the big silver wonder fish watching her. He had a big smile on his face. His silvery scales gleamed under the sun. The brightness of the fish dazzled her and she had to close her eyes from the brightness.

She started to dig again. There was a big splash. The spray of the water fell over her. She looked up to see the big silvery fish submerge and twist playfully in the water. Then he jumped again.

"You're showing off," Meriku scolded. He jumped again.

"Stop, I can't take time today. I have to fill this bucket," she said.

The salmon wanted to take her out for a spin on the bay but there was just no time.

The fish rode to shore on a wave. He made strange noises and as he did, the clams squeezed up through their holes and marched into the pail. It was a strange sight indeed. The salmon laughed.

"Now?" he asked.

Meriku put the bucket on the back of the fish and climbed aboard. It wasn't a very comfortable ride though as the clams became difficult. They stuck out their snouts and spit water over her.

Finally they reached the shore and the salmon stayed in hiding under the waves while Meriku delivered the clams to a fisherman to take to the house in the beach village.

The job finished, there was now time for fun. The little girl saw the salmon's shiny back arching between the swells of the sea. She raced out and jumped aboard. They rode the waves. She held on as the fish did his famous twist and jump. It was the most exciting ride that Meriku had ever had.

An Accident

The little girl heard a noise, and as she looked up, big tears ran down her cheeks. Then out of the woods came a big bull moose. Meriku was startled. She didn't know where to hide. She had heard stories about the bull moose, and how he chased and charged people with his great big horns.

She started to get up, but before she could, the big bull moose faced her near the tree stump. The little girl closed her eyes and waited. Nothing happened! She opened her big brown eyes, and saw the moose just standing and staring.

"You don't look cross," she muttered. The moose was silent.

"I'm lost. I'm cold and frightened. Please help me find my way back to my daddy." The moose just stood and stared.

"Please!" she cried. The big bull moose put down his head and Meriku held on to his big antlers and climbed on his back. They trotted through the forest, and finally they found where her father had been cutting. But there was no sign of him no matter how hard they looked.

 She was just about to give up when she heard a groan. Behind a tree was the form of a man on the ground. It was her daddy! He was hurt but he found enough strength to get on the bull-moose's back. They rode back to the village.

Meriku's daddy's got better with every day. When he recovered, he was surprised to see that the bull moose was still around. Meriku and the animal had become great friends. In fact, the bull-moose returned to the hunting grounds with Meriku and her Dad to help haul the Christmas trees to the Miramichi villages and towns.

> The bull moose brought a Christmas Tree, he brought it just for you and me
> He didn't even want a fee
> From us, his friends on the Miramichi

Naughty Muskrat

One day, the winter food supply was almost gone and Meriku's daddy decided to go back to the Miramichi brook to hook trout. He told the little girl she could join him. She brought along a slice of bread for a snack. Now that the bull moose had left for the back forest, they had to walk. By the time they reached the brook, Meriku was very tired and hungry. There was a little path through parts of the woods, but they often had to tramp through trees, pushing branches out of the way.

When they reached the brook, the water was running rapidly, splashing over the little pebbles as it ran. Meriku sat down while her father went further upstream. Meriku couldn't stay awake. She fell asleep stretched out on the slope above the brook. She slept for a good hour, and only awakened at the sound of a noise. She sat up, and there was a muskrat beating a trout against a rock. Then the animal went down the slope to the brook water, and washed the fish before he ate it.

The muskrat caught sight of the little girl. He crept up carefully and snooped around, looking for something a little different to eat. He was very saucy, and reached for Meriku's bread, and snatched it away before she could do anything about it!

"Don't! That's all I have!" she cried.

It was no use scolding, as by the time she had finished the words, the muskrat was down by the water washing the food. The bread got soggy, so much so, that it was hardly a mouthful for the animal. Tears came to the little girl's eyes, and rolled down her cheeks.

She followed the animal down the slope, and when he jumped into the water, she followed until they were both in midstream. The muskrat splashed, and caught several trout. He put them ashore, one by one. He was really showing off, and Meriku was getting impatient.

While the muskrat was busy fishing, the little girl went ashore and filled her 'kerchief with the fish. After all, the muskrat could get as many as he wanted, and wouldn't even miss them! Her father was delighted when Meriku returned with the trout. He had not been lucky with his catch.

On their return home, Meriku spotted the muskrat still playfully splashing in the water. She was sure he wouldn't miss his catch. The fish made a good swap for the bread.

Watching Birds

Spring was a quiet time in the Miramichi Mi'kmaq village. There wasn't very much for little girls to do. The snow had melted away, and the sleds couldn't be used. It was still too damp and cool for beach or water fun. The bull moose had taken off to the hunting grounds and it was ever so sad not to have him around. Meriku's mother said that the bull moose went back to find a mate. Meriku knew that the bull moose would soon have a family of his own, and he'd never really return to them again, at least not for keeps.

However, Meriku didn't stay sad too long. Like little girls do, she turned to something else. She took to bird watching. The sounds of the birds in the morning were like music to her ears. They chirped, chatted and sang. They greeted each day with such eagerness that Meriku woke up excited at the thought of a new day. The little birds came right up to her window, and if she didn't get up, they scolded. They were waiting for the suet and crumbs she threw out for feed every morning.

She watched them fly back and forth for a while before throwing food. When she approached the yard, they'd hide until she was out of sight again. They were very polite and not greedy. They lined up, allowing the larger ones to eat first. Perhaps it was in respect for their size that they waited. Maybe they weren't being polite at all. Nevertheless, they seemed most orderly.

One sunny morning, Meriku decided to sit outside and watch them feed. She wanted so much to be friendly. The birds were very timid. They were near and watching but they didn't trust the little girl. She sat for such a long time that the birds flew down and slowly crept closer to the crumbs. Finally, one found the courage to fly and land nearby. The other birds followed, realising that Meriku meant them no harm. In fact, in a few days they became so tame that they landed on the step right beside her.

This went on for weeks until one day Meriku went out and there were no birds in sight, only a little upturned nest. She turned the nest over and found a couple of blue speckled eggs. They were lovely. She was so pleased with the eggs that she had almost forgotten that something was wrong. She hid the eggs in the shed and waited. She decided to see what was wrong.

Maybe the winds were in a teasing mood. She put her arms up over her head but the wind that brushed against them was almost gentle. Maybe a storm was on its way. She looked up, searching the sky with her eyes. It was quiet; a blue sky with a few puffy white clouds drifting along. Everything looked calm. Her eyes searched the field and the trees.

Then she spotted a great big orange kite with a scary face on a tree branch. Meriku climbed the tree, removed it and placed it out of sight. She waited and the little birds arrived back. They were very excited, and seemed to be scolding. Meriku ran into the shed for the eggs, put them in the nest and climbed the tree again. Then she placed the nest, along with the spotted blue eggs, on the branch where the kite had been. The birds sang in a group, then scooped down one by one to the meal of torn bread waiting for them on the ground.

Search for a Gift

Birthdays were celebrated quietly in native villages. The families normally made their own gifts. Meriku gathered most of her gifts from nature, under the sun. Her mother's birthday was in May, in fact, it was today! The little Mi'kmaq girl combed the rocky shore looking for treasures but there wasn't even an unusual stone or shell to be found. Usually there was something among the sand and the stones when the beach was uncovered in the spring. Meriku felt sad at not having discovered a single item suitable for the occasion. She left the shore and walked sadly up the bank with her head cast down.

Suddenly, she remembered her lucky sand dollar! She ran home to get it and returned to the beach. She rubbed the sand dollar, looked out towards the water and in no time the huge silvery salmon was cruising towards her! The salmon looked shinier and brighter than ever, almost as if he had been re-scaled.

"Want to sail on my back?" he asked.

Meriku patted his silvery scales and looked into the salmon's blinking eyes. "Are there any sea treasures for a gift for my mother in the bay?" she asked.

"Hop on, and we'll find you a gift," he replied.

Meriku jumped on the salmon's back, and they skimmed over the water until they arrived at the colourful island. The salmon rested while the little girl searched the sandy beach. There was nothing suitable for a gift there. She walked through the little woods, and could see nothing but green fir trees.

Tears filled her big brown eyes and rolled out slowly down her chubby cheeks. The salmon must have been wrong. There were no gifts here.

All of a sudden, a fragrance saturated the air! It was beautiful. Only a mayflower could give off such an aroma! That's it, the gift for her mother! She looked under the big branch of the fir tree nearby, and in among the moss were hundreds of pink blooming flowers. She picked a big bunch and returned to the salmon, climbed aboard, and they sailed back to her home shore.

Empty Lobster Traps

Nature had blossomed afresh in June. It was Meriku's favourite month. Everything in Nature was so green. Cherry and apple blossoms bloomed and filled the air with its sweet-smelling scent. The birds loved June too, or so it seemed, as they were merrier than at any other time. They chirped, played and were on the move continuously, fluttering from tree to tree.

The bay also seemed livelier. The lobster traps were set for the season and one could just imagine underwater life being active as well. Meriku wandered down to the beach and looked out to see hundreds of markers floating on top of the water where the traps were set.

The lobsters didn't go for the bait this year and the fishermen in the village were very disappointed. They said lobster was scarce. This was hard to believe because Meriku had seen an army of them resting on the river bed in the bay inlet at the beginning of spring. Something must have happened. Lobsters were known to crawl slowly and maybe they just didn't make it to the bay in time for the season.

Meriku ran around the point to the little river, hoping the silver wonder-fish would come to her aid. She waited on the shore. There was no sign of the salmon. The fact it didn't come wasn't surprising, as salmon season was also open and the wonder fish kept busy in June, encouraging fish into the nets of good fishermen and keeping them out of nets owned by mean ones. The silver salmon knew a kindly face and a kindly person.

Nothing could fool him, even man. Meriku decided the problem was hopeless when a giant bull moose appeared up shore. The animal caught sight of Meriku and charged up the beach. The little girl didn't move. She knew it was Baby Moose now grown to full size. He was bigger and stronger than his father Bull Moose. He was so strong that he'd soon reign over animal life, not only in the hunting grounds, but in the whole Miramichi forests.

Meriku welcomed the moose and told him that the lobsters failed to come into the bay this year. She begged for help. Baby Moose agreed. He waded out into the little river, looking very clumsy and funny indeed. He was high in height and kept bending his head down into the water in search of the lobsters. He found them suddenly, and as if they knew his hoofs would trample them, they moved quickly, at a faster pace than lobsters were ever known to move, and marched into the bay water.

Baby Moose started to attract the attention of the villagers. He ran and disappeared quickly into the forest.

That evening the fishermen unloaded full traps. The lobsters had made for the bait and the villagers celebrated in song and dance.

The Raft

Logs drifted near the shore on Miramichi Bay. They had broken away from a boom. Meriku pulled them in with her father's long hook pole. She planned to make a raft and though it wasn't a girl's kind of job, she was determined to have a float boat of her own.

She pulled six logs onto the shore. The job of pulling them up the beach was an exhausting one, especially for one so little. She hid the logs in the wild sea wheat while she hunted for boards. Nearby she soon found enough materials for the float boat. Now it seemed only a matter of getting nails and a hammer to put it all together.

The horizon took on a combination of soft and vivid colours and a look of peace that only comes at twilight. To Meriku, it meant time to go home. Before going to bed, she told her father about the logs and her plans for a float boat. He didn't seem to mind. In fact, he gave her a bag of nails and a hammer to work with. The little girl found going to sleep difficult. The thought of owning a float boat ran through her mind.

The following morning she raced down to the shore and hauled the logs from the sea wheat and placed the boards across them. It was a bigger job than her thoughts had thought. It was awkward keeping the boards in place while she hammered. She needed help. She saw a group of her friends swimming at the nearby shelter. It was a little cove-like seashore place in the native village.

Meriku covered the logs and boards with branches so they wouldn't be discovered. She walked over to the shelter, waded in the water and joined the children. They splashed and played. Meriku could not swim and she ducked quickly, dress and all, because the water was cold but less painful when one got wet through. It was really lovely once in.

After the dip she challenged a boy, named Kutu, to a race. They ran down to the logs and when she stopped, she squeezed the water from her dress. She threw the branch aside and showed Kutu the unfinished float boat. He was eager to help. Meriku held the boards while he hammered before exchanging jobs. They worked all day and by evening until the float boat was finished. They'd meet in the morning at high tide, haul it to the breakers and set it afloat.

Meriku waited for Kutu at high tide. The village was very quiet. The dew was still on the grass and ground fog was low over the land. Meriku was happy. When Kutu arrived, he brought a thick rope with him. They tied it to the raft, and without much effort, it was in the water.

They jumped aboard pushing it out with a long pole. Kutu had brought an old anchor he had found on the upper beach. They had to go out a distance so that the float wouldn't be grounded at low tide. They decided to put down the anchor about half a mile out on the bay. Kutu took the anchor and tied it on the rope. He threw it into the water. But the the knot was too loose and the anchor came undone. There was no way of getting it again.

They floated along the waves. They couldn't haul the float ashore as the water was too deep. They drifted. Fortunately, there was an onshore wind or they would have been carried out to sea. The raft meandered around the cove to a quiet inland river.

When they neared shore, they jumped off. Meriku screamed. They had jumped into eel grass. The children felt the slimy snake-like eels brush against their legs. They boarded the float again and pushed themselves with the long pole away from the grass. The ground fog had lifted and the village seemed awake. They could see people walking around.

The feel of the sand beneath their feet was good. When float was safely tied, they decided to share it with everyone. They had a fisherman haul it around the bend and anchor it near the shelter for everyone to enjoy.

A Death

All was quiet in the native village on the Miramichi. It was past midnight and the people had settled in for the night. All of a sudden horrifying yells and moans echoed throughout the village. The cries were so loud that the villagers awoke one by one. After getting up and going to their windows, they watched an animal run wildly up and down the village road.

"It looks like a wild moose," yelled one villager to another.

They didn't dare move from their homes. From the sounds, a ferocious animal was on the loose. Meriku heard the commotion and when she looked out her bedroom window, she recognized the wild, noisy animal as none other than her old friend Bull Moose.

"It must be him," she thought, "and something dreadful must have happened to set him off on such a wild spree."

She pulled on her cardigan and ran down. Even though it was dark, the villagers recognised the figure of the little girl. They called her back. Meriku's own Daddy begged her to come back, telling her it wasn't the bull moose they knew, and even if it were it was in such a state that he could charge and kill her.

Meriku walked on. The bull moose cried and bucked. He headed towards the little girl. The villagers looking on and squealed with fear. They drew back from their windows dreading the thought of what might happen. The moose made a charge, stood up wildly on his hind legs, and let out a shrill cry. Suddenly, he landed on all four legs and faced Meriku quietly.

"You've been shot," she cried covering his big snout with kisses as she did so.

Meriku's daddy ran out to assist. He brought a light and a knife, intending to clean the wound, but the bull moose squealed at any attempt to help. He nudged the child gently. As if the nudge had been an invitation, they climbed on the back of the bull moose and headed towards the hunting grounds. He brought them to a thicket where a young moose lay resting.

The bull moose fell slowly to the ground. Meriku's Daddy cleaned the wound but it was useless. The animal had given up.

"We'll look after little bull moose," Meriku said with tears dripping in a steady stream.

Meriku's daddy tied a rope to the young moose and they began to lead him back to the village.

Finally at peace, the old bull moose closed his eyes in everlasting sleep.

Stories

An important looking man arrived in the Miramichi Mi'kmaq village. He came to collect village legends. Meriku wondered what the word legend meant. She asked her father and he explained that it was a story passed down over the years, a story retold from the days of the ancient chiefs.

No one in the village seemed friendly to the visitor who had arrived to collect stories of their people and their village. No one seemed to have a story. In fact, no one in the village seemed to trust him.

Meriku studied the man's face very carefully when he was around. He had a kind, friendly face. He wasn't asking for much, just a legend to take away with him. It seemed so little to give.

She remembered the stories her father had told her, stories that were told by grandfather chief long ago. She decided to sit on the shore as it was easier to think by the water than anywhere else. She sat on a big rock at the entrance of a small cave as it broke the force of the wind and also allowed the rays of the sun to reach her.

At first she didn't think at all. She just sat back and listened to the wind blow against the shelter of the cave. All at once, thoughts and stories came to mind, especially the story of how the Miramichi salmon came to be.

Many years ago, in the time of the princely chiefs, there lived a brave warrior named Salu. He was rich, owning a farm with healthy crops of grains and vegetables. There was game for meat in the forest and fish in the sea. Salu was the greatest hunter and the greatest fisherman in the native village. He always had plenty and always shared what he had with others.

This lasted until one hot summer when there was no rain and the sun dried the crops and the forest. Even the sea was different. It took on a dark, muddy look and strange fish appeared. They were monster like, with fire-like eyes and huge mouths with long sharp teeth. The fishermen were terrified and could no longer take their canoes out in the water. Soon there was so little food that the people were hungry. They begged Salu to help. He took his canoe and paddled out to sea spearing the monster fish as he drifted along. Soon the sea became pink with blood. The villagers called "Salu come", which sounded like salmon. Salu returned to the shore and the following day it rained, but too late to help the gardens or forest.

Since the water had changed to its normal colour and there were no sign of the giant monster fish in the sea, Salu canoed out, followed by his friends, and caught fish for food.

When they had them prepared, they discovered the flesh was pink instead of flower white. They cooked the fish over open fires. They were the tastiest fish they had ever eaten. And like the sound of the word that came out for "Salu come", they named the fish salmon after the brave warrior Salu.

Meriku ran and found the white man and told him the story of the Miramichi salmon and how it came to be.

The Moose Call

There were two festivals close to each other in Mi'kmaq Village. One was St. Anne's Picnic. It was held outside in the grounds of the little white wooden church with the tall steeple. There was a bazaar and cake sale. The blueberry pie was delicious. Lots of different booths had games to play. Meriku won a teddy bear there once. The next festival was a pow wow. Meriku liked the traditional costumes, the dancing and chanting. There was lots of food and a big bonfire at night. Someone always had fireworks. Visitors came and stayed in the village for a few days.

During one of these week-ends, Meriku met an old man sitting on a rock where the beach came to a point. It was sunset. The sky was ribbons of pink and purple. The man was watching blue herons as they fished in the bay. They would stand on one leg, still and silent for a long time. In a flash, their pointed beaks would stab at the water and come up with a shiny, silvery fish.

The old man started making strange noises. Meriku sat beside him, staying quiet to listen. After awhile, she thought she recognised one of the sounds. A group of seagulls was flying madly over head, squawking and arguing with each other. The man's noises blended in with their confusion.

Meriku felt something fall onto her shoulder. She jumped up. It was seagull droppings. She took a tissue out of her pocket and wiped it off. Then she waved her arms to shoo away the seagulls.

"Those birds are always trouble. Can't you make any other sounds?" she asked.

The old man looked as if he were smiling although his mouth did not move. His wise old eyes beamed through his crinkled tanned skin. Then his mouth went to work in a series of whistles, sighs and other sounds that brought to life the image of the forest on a hot summer's day. Birds chirped, uttered and held single notes, bees buzzed, wings flapping against the air. The little girl jumped with excitement.

"You are magic", she said.

"Nature is magic," said the old man, breaking his silence with words. "Now for something really special".

He held out his hands as if clutching the handle bars of a bicycle. He then closed both hands to make a loose fist. He brought the left fist to his mouth and then brought the right fist to fit at the end of the first one. He twisted the two fists like he was trying to adjust a telescope. He then blew in through the fingers. The sound he made was loud, powerful and eerie. She had never heard such a thing before and was very impressed.

"I will teach you," said the old man.

"What sound is it?" asked Meriku.

"You will see," he said.

The old man positioned her hands and showed her how to blow. Meriku turned red from blowing but she could not manage any sound. As if he had all the time in the world, the old man kept repositioning her hands and giving instructions. After many, many attempts, Meriku blew an enormous sound. She fell back surprised at her own power.

"What was that?" she asked. "I have never heard a bird like that before."

The old man was silent, listening. Then there was a crashing sound over by where the river comes out of the forest and flows into the sea. The little girl stared in expectation.

Then - out stepped grown-up "Baby Bull Moose". He looked around in surprise, wondering who had called him. When he saw Meriku, he went up and nuzzled her shoulder. He smiled, the way moose do. The old man started to smile too. Then Meriku joined in the fun.

Meriku had thought that Baby Bull Moose had been avoiding her. She had promised to watch over the young animal when his father died but lately could not get in touch with him. He nudged her to get up on his back. They left the old man and headed towards the forest.

"Now I can contact you anytime," said Meriku as she put her arms around the animal's neck.

Mirimichi Pete
of the River Bank

How Pete Gets His Name

Pete Owleye hated his name. He was ashamed because the name 'Owl-eye' brought a curious look from grown-ups and the word 'Owl' made children laugh and tease.

"Hoot, hoot," they would say.

Pete lived on a farm near the bank of the Miramichi River. This he liked because his favourite pastime was fishing, and next to fishing, he liked to watch the big ships go up and down the river, especially at night, when they looked like big, beautiful hotels.

One day Pete came down to the river just to cry. He cried because he was lonely and shy. He cried because he had no friends. His name made him feel that way. Who would want to know an 'Owl'? If Pete only knew that many children might like and enjoy the little boy behind the name! Children had often tried to be friendly but Pete had always shied away.

He stopped crying and played with the cones that had fallen from the big pines. He listened to the sounds of nature: to the bird songs, the rustle of the leaves, the splash of the fish and to the whistle of the ships on the river.

Suddenly he heard voices and footsteps coming in his direction. He ran and hid on the side of the bank. He was not there very long when he got tired of having to squat on slippery sandy soil. The wiggly rock he was holding on to suddenly gave way and Pete felt himself slide down into the river.

"Help! Help!" he cried. Splash!

He went into the cold water.

A man jumped in, grabbing Pete, and brought him back to shore. Another man helped the boy up the bank.

"What's your name?" the man asked.

"Pete", he answered.

"Miramichi Pete," the man laughed in fun at the wet boy.

"Miramichi Pete", the boy echoed.

The name made him feel important and brave. He told all the boys and girls his new name. "Miramichi Pete" was the name he got from that day forward, and he never felt lonely again.

An Old Friend In Trouble

Miramichi Pete's troubles didn't completely end with the finding of a new name. He liked horses. There were two on the farm where he lived, 'Appleye' and 'Saucy'. Appleye was the boy's favourite. Being smaller, Mirimichi Pete felt well on his back.

One day the boy overheard his father say that the horses would have to be sold. He had new machines to take their place. Miramichi Pete was very sad. He ran to the barn and over to Appleye. The horse bent his head and nuzzled the boy playfully. Pete stroked Appleye's head gently and as he did, big tears came to the little boy's eyes and rolled slowly down his cheeks.

Suddenly he had an idea! He would take Appleye into the woods and down to the river. He led the horse from the barn over to the fence and climbed onto his back. They rode happily through the fields to a path in the forest. A moose-jay followed them when they reached the woods. However, somehow the wooded path didn't seem wide enough for the horse and the boy. Maybe they were too high or too wide. Tree branches were in the way as they passed.

Horses have a way of telling us when they are unhappy. Appleye stopped and shook his head sideways, making sneezing noises like horses do when they don't like something.

"Never mind, we'll turn back," the boy said.

It wasn't easy turning because Appleye didn't want to get brushed by the scratchy branches again. Miramichi Pete gave an extra hard tug of the reins and the horses made a quick turnabout. Not caring now, he galloped along the narrow path to the clearing.

Miramichi Pete felt the scratches on his face as they rode through the field to the highway. The boy pulled the reins tightly to bring the animal to a halt. The highway was busy with traffic. It was noisy with the sound of engines and tooting of horns.

Appleye made nervous, sneezing sounds again. He tried to move away. He was very frightened. When the highway was clear, Appleye wouldn't even move with the extra tug of the reins. Pulling one rein brought Appleye to a full turn and back towards the farm.

The boy's daddy was waiting at the farmyard. He was angry, but when Pete told him why he had taken Appleye away, his Daddy changed his mind and said that Appleye could remain on the farm with them. Miramichi Pete was happy again.

Perils of Autumn

Satisfied that Appleye would remain on the farm, Pete relaxed, and there was no better place for real relaxing than in the forest. Mr. Owleye warned Pete not to go to the woods during October. There were men with guns behind big spruce trees. These men, his Daddy said, were hunting deer and partridge and often shot at little sounds and movements. It was a dangerous time of year.

But staying at home, Miramichi Pete missed the songs of the birds. He missed the smell of the spruce. He missed searching for little treasures of the forest. He often collected moss, leaves or berries, the kind of things not found on the farm.

Miramichi Pete stood and looked at the forest. He started to walk, and before he even thought, he was walking towards the old stream. The stream had become a pond. There were beavers swimming in it, carrying sticks between their teeth. They looked so busy and didn't even see Miramichi Pete. They were building something that made the water rise. He threw a pebble, but the beavers worked on as if whatever they were doing had to be done at that very minute.

A brown rabbit ran into the clearing. When he saw the boy, he stopped, sat on his hind legs and perked his ears as rabbits do when taken by surprise. Then it ran quickly back into the woods.

Miramichi Pete heard a song. He left the busy beavers to follow it, but as he did, bullets shot past his ear. He only then remembered his father's warning! The sounds of gunshot were loud. Miramichi Pete hid behind a tree. He heard footsteps. Then he saw two men with guns, and as they passed, he called out for help. The men looked saw Miramichi Pete with big tears flowing down his cheeks.

He was lucky. The two men were friendly. They even walked the boy back to the farm. Miramichi Pete decided that his Daddy was right. The woods were no place for little boys in October.

Winter Water Adventure

Miramichi Pete laughed when he saw the big mountain of snow in the farmyard. He climbed up, pulling his new toboggan behind him. The snow had hardened just right for sliding. He lay on his tummy and down he slid. It was so much fun! He slid down and walked up a dozen times.

Like most little boys, he grew tired of being in one place for too long, so he decided to find a bigger mountain of snow. He walked across the road to the river bank. The bank was very steep and Miramichi Pete began to worry that it was too high. He placed his toboggan facing the frozen over river and screwed up the courage to start.

There was a ship stuck in the ice below and an ice-breaker had arrived to help break it away. Miramichi Pete watched the little boat work through the ice. He got on the toboggan, forgetting about the steep bank, and gave himself a push with one foot. The toboggan went down the slope at such a great speed that Miramichi Pete had to hold on very tight. He tried to drag his foot to slow the speed, but the toboggan sped on, and before anything could be done, Miramichi Pete found himself almost in midstream.

The little tug-like boat kept coming forward. The ice started to crack, Miramichi Pete found himself on a little island of ice. He called out and waved at the big ship. He called out and waved at the little icebreaker. No one saw or heard the little boy. Miramichi Pete cried. He was cold and frightened. He couldn't even try to swim. It would be dangerous in the freezing water. He might even get caught under the ice if he tried.

"Help!" Miramichi Pete yelled. His voice got tired and his arms were sore from waving.

'They would never see him,' he thought, they were all too busy getting the big ship out to the channel. He would be left to freeze. Poor little Miramichi Pete!

The boy danced up and down to keep moving as much as he could against the cold. Suddenly, he saw a rubber boat being thrown over the side of the big ship. A rope ladder was thrown over and a sailor climbed down to the ice below.

"Ahoy!" Mirimichi Pete yelled.

No one replied. Then a sailor grabbed the rubber boat and carried it across the ice to the open water.

"He's coming! He's coming!" Mirimichi Pete cried in delight.

He climbed eagerly into the little boat, shivering. The sailor took him to the wheel room and gave the boy some hot tea. The captain radioed ashore to send news that Miramichi Pete was aboard. The little boat could not take him ashore until later, but Miramichi Pete was now warm and dry, and enjoying his first sail through the river ice.

Sleigh Ride

The snow was firm and cold. Miramichi Pete felt bored. He went skating. He went sliding. However, the cold forced him indoors. The snow froze to his mittens and he shivered. He went to the kitchen, opened the range oven door and put up his legs to warm and thaw out. The boy's mother brought him a crust of freshly baked bread and molasses along with a cup of hot milk. His mother's bread tasted best just out of the oven.

Little boys get restless and Miramichi Pete grew tired of staying in. His clothes were dry and warm again so he decided to hitch his horse to his new red sleigh, and ride around the farm. His mother didn't like the idea as it was such a cold day, but the boy was determined. He took his mother's big bear rug to put over himself.

After the boy hitched the horse to the sleigh, he added bells to Appleye's harness. He could hardly wait to get started, to hear them jingle! They rode over to the next farm to pick up his friend Patti. The bells tingled just as he had hoped they would. They sounded beautiful.

Patti must have heard them coming because she waved from the window. She put her outdoor clothes on in a hurry and ran out. She brought along a red bow and tied it to the harness next to the horse's face. Mirimichi Pete hopped out of the sleigh to inspect it. They both laughed. Appleye had never looked so beautiful!

They were snug and warm under the bear rug in the sleigh, and feeling very proud of Appleye, they decided he should be seen by all. They headed into town on the main highway. The going was not good, as the snow was worn down by traffic. Appleye felt the weight of the sleigh and couldn't gallop along as freely as usual.

"Giddiup! Giddiup! Giddiup!" Pete urged the horse.

"That's not right. The road is almost bare," Patti protested. The horse moved slowly until he had almost slowed down to barely a walk. The boy stood up and jiggled and jiggled the reins. "You're cruel, Miramichi Pete. All you care about is showing Appleye off. You don't really care about him at all," the girl scolded.

The boy saw a side road that led to a back road to the farm. He turned off, and as soon as the horse's hooves reached the hard-packed snow, he started off in a gallop again. They both laughed and it became a happy sleigh ride again for all.

A Special Gift

Miramichi Pete was excited about Christmas. He wanted everything in sight. He visited the shops and looked at toy soldiers, helmets, games, cars and an assortment of every kind of toy imaginable. He expected and even bragged that Santa would bring him all these things on Christmas day. Friends warned him not to be so greedy, but Miramichi Pete laughed in reply.

It wasn't like Miramichi Pete to want so much, but the look of all those toys made him forget everything else. He wanted them all.

"A whole mountain of toys," he boasted to everyone within hearing reach.

It was sad what Christmas was doing to Miramichi Pete.

Still fevered with the excitement of Christmas, the boy went out to the woods with an axe to fell a tree. He walked along the narrow path in the forest. He passed a number of healthy little trees but shook his head in disapproval. Suddenly Pete caught sight of the tree he wanted. It was the tallest tree in the forest.

As he began chopping with his axe, the little bushy trees sighed as they rocked back and forth in the wind. Pete chopped and chopped, then wiped his forehead. He grew tired and sat down. He wasn't making any progress with the big tree.

Miramichi Pete gave up and started for home when the little bushy trees closed in on him.

"Please, I have to get through. I want to go home", he pleaded.

The bushy little trees didn't move. Tears came to his eyes and he muttered that he was sorry. The trees moved away.

"You want the biggest and the most of everything. One of us little bushy trees would be happy to be yours"

"You're right, Thank-you."

Miramichi Pete chose one, chopped it and dragged it home carefully. He dressed it beautifully with painted pinecones, bright ribbon and candy canes.

He forgot all about his mountain of toys. He was too busy and too happy at the sight of the decorated tree. Even if Santa didn't come because he had been greedy, the boy knew he had enough by just remembering the true meaning of Christmas.

Santa did come to the Owleye farm at Christmas. In fact, he left a lot more than Pete had expected. The boy had secretly hoped for a Raven King figure, the star of his favourite cartoon. After being so greedy, he hadn't liked to tell anyone. Nevertheless, he couldn't help feeling a wee bit disappointed.

On his way to the forest on Christmas morning, he brought Appleye a special treat of delicious apples and sugar lumps. Then he went on his way. Thinking of the Raven King, he forgot to bring his snowshoes along. It was hard-going and with each step, he sank deeply. It took him longer than he ever remembered to get to his little camp in the woods. He was almost breathless when he arrived.

The camp-house was cold and bleak and he felt sorry that he had left the warmth of his home and his sparkling little tree. After all, it was Christmas day. Not able to stand the bleakness any longer, he started to walk home.

On his way, to make everything seem stranger, he kept hearing a "caw caw" sound. He looked backwards and sideways, but there was nothing to be seen. The sound followed him with each step. Spotting a log, he decided to have a rest. The "caw caw" sound grew louder.

Then he saw a big bird swoop down and land on the log beside him. It was a shiny blue-black in colour, just like the Raven King figure he dreamed of having. But this was no figure. It was very real.

The bird flapped its wings. Pete turned to examine it. Around the neck was a disc and on it in fine print was written:

"Merry Christmas, Miramichi Pete".

Santa had remembered after all. The Raven was his very own. Pete whistled as he walked on with the Raven close by. Once back at the farm, he brought the Raven into the barn.

At first, Appleye made a fuss. But then, as if he realized he'd be sharing his shelter with the bird from then on, he calmed down and Pete's two favourite creatures agreed to share the shelter from then on.

Winter Carnival

It was winter carnival time. Miramichi Pete had never attended a carnival before. It had snowed during the week, the temperature took a dip downwards and the sun was bright: just the right conditions for a winter celebration. The highway was firmly parked with snow, making it possible to take Appleye out for a trot. Pete dressed the horse up with his special red harness, bow and bells, for the occasion.

They rode into town. As they went through the streets, people cheered and waved as Appleye trotted by. Miramichi Pete could see his breath as he sat holding the reins. It was very cold, but he was warmly dressed. Besides, he had a buffalo robe to pull over him just in case. The frost was just nippy enough to pinch the cheeks of boys and girls to bring out a rosy, healthy glow.

Everyone looked happy. The Miramichi had never seen so many smiling faces all at once. Maybe the cold tickled their humour, or maybe it was Appleye's bells that tickled them.

"That's what it is," he thought, and felt proud.

They trotted up to the schoolyard to see the students' snow sculptures. Miramichi Pete brought Appleye to a halt, hopped off and made for a ship made of snow. He boarded it. The frosty air made the snowboat firm enough to hold him seated.

Then he heard Appleye call, the way horses call that is. He jumped off and ran over to see the horse surrounded by boys and girls. Appleye, being naturally shy, didn't like all the attention. In fact, he was frightened. Pete could always tell, as the horse's eyes always look sideways and shifty when he was nervous. Pete pushed the children aside and gave the horse a confident pat. He stroked his nose until Appleye's eyes focused back to a normal state.

The children begged for a sleigh ride. It wasn't possible to take them all so Mirimichi Pete decided to charge ten cents and take five at a time, making it 50 cents a ride. This was so successful that in no time Pete had made five dollars, the largest amount of money he'd ever had. He took the money and went downtown, hitching Appleye to a parking meter. He went into a shop and bought sugar lumps for the horse. The rest would be used to buy wading boots for spring fishing.

When Pete brought back the sugar, Appleye was hopping up and down. He shook his head in a terrible state. Someone had pinned a piece of paper to his harness and it hung over his right eye. The boy soon discovered that it was a parking ticket. Appleye looked exhausted. There were so many people, so many cars and then to have a ticket pinned over his eye. It was too much for a horse.

Miramichi Pete directed the horse to the police station and knocked at the door while holding on to the reins. He couldn't leave Appleye alone again. Miramichi Pete explained to the officer that Appleye was a very sensitive horse.

"It might take him months, even years, to get over his trip to town," Pete explained.

The policeman's face broke into a smile. He patted the horse and told them to be on their way, warning them not to forget to feed the meter next time.

As usual, as on most outings with Appleye, getting settled back on the farm was a comforting feeling.

Fire

It was a nasty day. The sun wasn't out and the cold wind blew hard. Miramichi Pete didn't like the force of the wind. Its strength made it difficult for him to walk. He decided to play Boy Scout. He got his hammer, his hatchet and nails from the barn and put snowshoes on as the snow was deep in the field. The narrow path in the woods was covered with snowdrifts.

Miramichi Pete was going to build a house made of boughs at the edge of the forest. He cut tree stems and leaned the narrow lengths of wood against the fence dividing the field and forest. He cut boughs and covered the top. It was difficult as the wind was against him and the snow was so soft; it was hard to get a firm grip.

Miramichi Pete decided to camp out in his bough house. The following day, he harnessed Appleye and put his camp supplies on the sleigh. Patti arrived just in time to join him and they started off. Appleye galloped until he reached the middle of the field. The soft deep snow made the going bad for the horse; he had to wade through it.

Patti was delighted when she saw what Pete had done. They left the supplies on the sled. Miramichi Pete shovelled snow away from the lean-to. He took the bear rug and laid it on the ground. He had thought of everything. He had even brought matches and kindling for a fire. The fire was laid. It burned slowly.

The children decided that perhaps more wood was necessary. Miramichi Pete placed boughs on the fire, making a high pile, and Patti sat down to enjoy her sandwich. The pile caught fire and flames seemed to go every which way. Patti moved quickly and called to Pete. The boy ran over to the bough house and pulled out the rug. Within minutes, the lean-to was gone.

Miramichi Pete felt bad about the loss of the wooden structure and because the fire was so dangerous, he decided he'd never start one again so close to trees.

Crossing the River

Miramichi Pete added more bells to Appleye's harness. They jingled as he trotted along the highway. They were going to cross the bridge spanning the river. The bridge led to other towns and villages of the Miramichi.

The horse trotted proudly and the boy sat holding the reins loosely between his hands. It would be the first time that Appleye had ever been on a bridge.

On approaching it, the horse slowed down to a slow walking pace. The cars and heavily loaded trucks made him nervous. The drivers gave him that kind of uppity look, the "you don't belong" one that some people have when they think there is an intrusion. Appleye looked straight at them. Then he raised his head in a haughty way as if to say it was more his bridge than theirs.

He smartened up and began to trot again. He didn't even slow down at the sight of a huge truck coming his way.

But then Appleye started to tremble as the wagon shook in the wake of the truck. Miramichi Pete shook, so much so he was still shaking when they reached the other side. Appleye had lost his smart stride. In fact, he looked rather haggard. His pace was so slow that the bells on his reins hardly tinkled at all.

Miramichi Pete swung the reins over and directed the horse to a side road along the river. Appleye calmed down as they stopped in time to see a ship approach. The bridge draw opened and the vessel started to pass through. Somehow, as if too large for the opening, it struck the side with a bang. The bridge was broken.

Miramichi Pete wondered how he'd ever get back to the other side. Appleye's eyes filled with tears. The boy had never seen a horse with real tears in his eyes before.

Maybe they could swim, he thought, but then Pete remembered that in the cool waters of April, it was hardly likely. They trotted through the villages to the little branches of the river until they found a bridge.

They crossed and Appleye trotted at a quick nervous pace through the darkness until they reached the farm. Never did the solid ground of the farm fields feel so good.

Miramichi Pete decided his horse was best kept in the farm fields and open spaces and to only allow him to view the other side of the river from where he was.

Bad Water

Miramichi Pete decided to take Appleye and go to the salmon stream. The horse hadn't been off the farm for months and the boy wasn't sure how the animal would react to being on the highway again. The highway led to the stream. Pete knew he had promised not to take the horse on busy roads but it would only be for a short way.

Once off, Appleye trotted along at a good pace. The boy knew the horse was timid and really nervous of the passing cars. When they reached the cut-off to a narrow dirt road that led to the stream, the horse broke into a run, happy to be on farm-like ground again.

Settled beside the stream, the horse took to nibbling grass while the boy prepared his fishing gear. He noticed that the water had somehow changed in the stream. It had a dull, soupy look and dust seemed to float on its surface. Even its mood seemed different; it was very still, lending an unhappy look to the whole scene.

There was so little movement that the boy wondered whether any salmon still remained in the once merry stream. He decided to cast his line hoping to get a bite. No such luck however. He sat until the sun lowered in the sky, telling him that the day had almost ended. It was time to leave. He pulled in his line and as he did a salmon appeared.

The salmon didn't want the bait. It opened and closed his mouth, looking sadly at the film of the water. Suddenly, the fish bravely swam up and nudged the boy and didn't stop until Pete waded into the water. The fish jumped and dove onto the stream.

Miramichi Pete knelt and looked down to discover the sea plants had wilted and small fish lay dead on the sandy bottom. Industrial waste had destroyed them. The little stream had been popular. People had picnicked nearby but had also thrown bottles, old food waste and dirt into the water. Now it was sick.

The boy decided it was not too late to save the precious little stream. He left his fishing gear on the farm and returned daily to clean up. He worked until the little stream became its merry self again. It twinkled in the sunlight and new life appeared in its depths.

Miramichi Pete sighed and then sang, "twinkle go, twinkle come" to the little stream of fun. The salmon jumped. It was ready for business. Miramichi Pete was too. He took out his fishing line, knowing that the fishing game was truly on.

Freak Weather

Miramichi Pete dreamed of streams and jumping trout. It was Saturday morning and he was now eager to go to the forest stream. He could hear the birds chatter loudly outside his bedroom window. He looked out and to his surprise, the month of May had either jumped backwards or far forwards season wise. The roof, the trees and the ground were covered with snow. It was bewildering that May would present such a temperamental display of weather. The birds chattered and fluttered and seemed most frustrated by the intrusion of snow. The plumpest bird, Mr. Robin, had just arrived from the South to summer on the Miramichi.

Mr. Robin was usually very quiet and usually very happy. Now he was upset and Pete could tell that Mr. Robin was beginning to think that possibly for the first time he had made a mistake in the seasons.

Pete pulled the curtains open, got dressed and hurried out, not even taking time out for breakfast. He had to convince Mr. Robin it was truly May. He broke a branch off a tree and called the bird. Mr. Robin hopped on the roof, then flew over and perched on the branch and studied the little buds. For the first time since his arrival, he went quiet. The boy took his fishing tackle and hiked to the stream. The forest around him seemed livelier and there were sounds of excitement. He left his tackle when he reached the water and went to investigate.

In a small clearing there was a family of rabbits scolding and talking at once. They were trying to wiggle out of their new brown coats. Further on in the woods, a family of bears quarrelled. They scolded one another and blamed each other for getting up to soon out of their winter sleep. The squirrel family didn't take time out to argue. They scampered back to their little tree home, just peeking out occasionally to check on their surroundings. The intrusion of winter in May had upset the whole animal kingdom.

Pete returned to his tackle and when he arrived at the stream, the water was its cheery self. It splashed and flowed merrily over its rocky bottom. The only difference was that the trout seemed livelier. They just didn't stay still at all and Pete knew they were too restless to catch, too excited even to take time out for a nibble.

Miramichi Pete wished he could help. Unlike people who just look at a calendar to know what month it was, the animals and fish followed their instincts when it came to knowing when a new season had arrived. This had gone astray with the unsuspected snow.

The boy stood, thinking. His thoughts seemed to be out of proportion to the size of his head. The thoughts could measure around on the outside comfortably but inside there were too many to be pleasant. Suddenly up popped one thought that seemed to fit the problem.

Miramichi Pete walked over into the woods. He swept the snow aside under the big spruce branches and uncovered a mayflower. Then he made a little brush from twigs and began to sweep all round, uncovering more and more flowers.

The fragrance of the beautiful pink flowers latched on to a breeze and blew through the forest. All sounds became still. The birds and animals sniffed and followed the scent to find the Mayflower in bloom. Life in the forest was restored to its natural order.

Forest Fire

Patti and Pete were on their way to the forest, but in front of them was a big smoke cloud. It hovered over their beloved woods, still and eerie. Miramichi Pete took hold of Patti's hand and started to run, pulling her along as he did.

"It's a fire!" he yelled. "Hurry up, we have to help the animals!"

Patti started running, but as they approached the wood, smoke filled their lungs. They could smell nothing else. It was so dreadful that Patti began to choke a little. Then they heard crashing and banging, and saw that animals were running in terror out of the forest they had called home.

They had an idea, and hurried home again, keeping watch for approaching animals. They could hear the sound of hoofs and the cries of a forest in distress. When they arrived at the farm, the boy hitched the cart to Appleye and Patti filled buckets with water. One deer who had followed them was so thirsty that he drank one of the buckets dry.

The children loaded the wagon with water and food scraps, then jumped aboard and headed back to the forest. They could see the red of the flames now. The fire was getting worse. Miramichi Pete had sense enough to know that two children and the wagon's water supply could be of little use in fighting it. The water could be used instead for the thirsty animals. They took an old wash tub, filled it with water and left it at the edge of the forest. They went back and forth keeping the tub filled, while many animals stopped gratefully to have a little drink in their flight.

When the job was done, they lay back on the hay field exhausted. Patti had almost gone off to sleep when she heard a splash. She sat up quickly and there in the tub was a raccoon cooling off.

"You naughty animal," she cried.

They headed home, feeling their job was done for the day. The sunset in the sky was scarlet. Pete's father stood facing their beloved forest, watching and wondering. There were clouds in the sky, but they wouldn't cry. The tears of the sky were spent.

Priscilla Simms
of Beach Village

A Friend In The House

Beach Village looked lonelier than ever. There wasn't a sign of life to be seen or heard. The only indication that someone might be there was grey smoke coming out of the white house beyond the road. The other houses along the beach were boarded up.

In the white house beyond the road, a lonely little girl played "make believe". Her name was Priscilla Simms. She pretended that she was a mommy and dressed in grown-up clothes and high heels. She couldn't go out to play because she was getting over a fever and a cold.

Her daddy worked at the lumber camps in the woods at this time of year. He only came home during the weekends. Priscilla missed him, though she understood why he had to be away. He needed money to keep his family and the Miramichi mills needed him to cut trees. Lumber was needed everywhere for building.

Priscilla often went to the edge of the woods and watched lumber being hauled out on sleds and then loaded on trucks for delivery. She felt proud to think that her daddy had a part of such an important operation. The best part of her daddy's being away was his coming home. Each week he brought stories of life and happenings in the lumber camp.

Priscilla took off her dress-up clothes. She wished that she could go out. She had been sick and now her mother was down with a fever too. Priscilla went to the window and spotted her friend the Canadian Goose. He was being very playful, flying up and gliding down. She went to the door and called him. He glided down and landed beside her. The little girl gave him a big hug.

"I'm going to bring you into the house." She pulled and the goose objected. He squawked.

"Don't you like houses?" she asked.

The goose seemed frightened. Priscilla got a hold on its leg. It flapped its big wings, hitting the little girl so hard that she fell into the doorway. The goose fell in after her. The little girl got up quickly and closed the door.

"Honk!"

"Sh, Shhhh! " she warned. The goose walked around. It became very timid and quiet. It had never been in a house before. The little girl took out her dress-up clothes and dressed the goose.

It didn't squawk. At first, it tried to wiggle out of the clothes. Then it just waddled around, cute in a little dress, shawl and hat. They played and Priscilla was having so much fun that she forgot the time. She began to feel hungry and her hunger made her think of the time. It was supper time and Mrs. Simms was still in bed.

Priscilla went upstairs. Her mother looked very sick and her head was very hot. Priscilla left very quietly and went back downstairs. She found crackers, peanut butter and milk. She put a dish on the floor for the goose and was just about to eat when she heard a noise in the hall. She ran out and found her mother on the floor. Priscilla tried to get her mother to speak but there was no response.

She tried using the telephone but there was no answer so she put on her warm clothes and went out, taking the goose with her. She climbed on his back and they flew a mile to the nearest house for help. The lady of the house, Mrs. Ready, drove Priscilla back home. Mrs. Ready was strong enough to lift Mrs. Simms up and put her on the couch. Mrs. Simms came to. She was very weak but she was going to be alright. Mrs. Ready made a pot of hot soup for them. It was delicious.

Priscilla heard a noise at the back door. She opened it and in walked the Canadian Goose. They both laughed.

"This is my new friend," said Priscilla, smiling.

The Perfect Leaf

The forest beyond Beach Village was aglow with colour. They were such lovely warm colours that Priscilla Simms decided to tell her mommy to use them indoors the next time a room needed to be painted.

The colours were so bright and so beautiful from where she stood! The leaves themselves couldn't be seen in the distance, only the outline of the trees. Priscilla went into the house for her mother's scissors and then headed towards the woods. As she came closer she could see the branches.

She ran and grabbed the point of a branch which hung down near the trunk of the tree. Looking at the leaves very closely, they didn't look as bright or as perfect as they did from a distance. She ran from tree to tree until she found a perfect branch. She tried cutting but the scissors were either too dull or the branches too thick and she finally used her hands to break one off.

Under the broken branch, on another little branch, a little squirrel swung up and over, up and over. Up and over it went again. It was acting more like a monkey than a squirrel. It stopped, bowed and went up and over again. A chattering, scolding noise came from another branch of the tree. That was probably the mother squirrel as Priscilla could see her bushy tail.

The little one ignored the scolding and continued his game of going up and over. He was so playful.

The girl then heard a squeal. The playful squirrel had lost its balance and fallen. He rested on the ground very quietly. Priscilla looked for the mother but she was out of sight. She picked him up so he wouldn't be prey for larger animals and walked deeply in the forest, poking her head into tree trunk openings as she went along, only to be scolded away by other squirrel families living there.

She was just about to give up when she found a free place in a tree. She made a bed of leaves and soft moss and a coverlet of fern and placed it in the tree. Knowing how much squirrels liked nuts, she went back to her house and picked a handful of soft green nuts from the linden tree in the front yard. She ran back to the forest and placed them in with the squirrel. It ate a few and she left for home.

The following day she started out for the woods to visit the squirrel but before she reached the woods, she noticed a family of squirrels near the linden tree. They had come to make a home there. What a lovely home it was for them with the soft green shell nuts and the lovely bushy branches to hide in. The squirrels hid when they heard her coming, all except the little playful one. She suspected that he had given up his silly ways. He just smiled, the way squirrels do that is. Then he scampered away to join his family.

Halloween Games

The children in Beach Village on the Miramichi celebrated Halloween night, not unlike the way children do in other places. The only difference was that in Beach Village one had to work to get treats by dunking for apples placed in a tub of water.

Priscilla Simms practiced so much that her hair was wet most of the time and she felt a cold coming on. Though she had almost become an expert at dunking and bringing up an apple between her teeth, she felt herself becoming sick. She just had to go out! If not, it would be her very first Halloween night on her own.

She tried coughing quietly into her pillow at night. But it was of no use as it became so bad that she coughed in her sleep. Her mother heard everything, which meant that Halloween would be spent in bed. She felt sad. She could hear the doorbell ring continuously and the sound of the children's' excitement. Her own costume hung on the back of her bedroom door, a witch's dress made by her mother for the occasion. She felt sleepy and, as her eyes fought sleep, the little costume seemed to take on a form and come alive.

Priscilla felt she couldn't stay awake a moment longer. Suddenly, the costume fell off the door and a little witch appeared. She was cute and friendly. She smiled and was not the way Priscilla imagined witches to be.

"How many houses would you have visited tonight?" she asked.

"At least five," Priscilla replied.

"You'll get five treats," said the witch.

The witch swirled and spoke magic words, swooped down and then up with a jewelled crown. This was the first treat. Priscilla put it on her head. It was beautiful.

The witch swirled and spoke again and this time, a golden bucket full of candy appeared. This was followed by a bracelet, a white bunny coat and a party dress. They were lovely, not at all like treats given on Halloween.

Her head felt hot. She could hear her mother's voice. She was coming into the room carrying an armful of treats the village children had brought when they learned Priscilla was sick. The witches treats were gone, nowhere to be found. It didn't matter. She had candy apples, peanuts and sweets. It was much more than she would have had if she had gone trick-or treating-herself. Priscilla felt that it was the best Halloween night she had ever known.

Helping a Friend

The November frosts had cooled Miramichi Bay to an icy temperature. The salmon swam to and fro for their late Autumn voyage to the ocean. Soon the cold would cause ice to form on the bay. If they didn't leave, they'd be trapped for the winter. None of the fish wanted to be caught or left behind.

Priscilla Simms gathered stones on the beach. She used little flat ones to make neck pendants. Making jewellery kept her busy during the long winter on the bay. The water felt icy, so much so that she had to withdraw her hands quickly and rub them together.

Hearing a splash, she looked up and saw the silver wonder fish jump out of the water. She ran along the shore until she reached the wharf where she sat on the slip. The water was calm and she could see the salmon swim by in rows, the silver wonder fish directing them on their way.

The leader led pool after pool of fish out to the sea. Priscilla watched fascinated by their energy. She stayed until the sun went down. As she reached the steps leading from the beach up to the road to her home, she heard strange noises. However when she looked, there was nothing to be seen.

The noise grew louder and she followed it to the nearest little wave. The head of a fish popped out of the wave. It was a salmon and tears appeared to roll out of its blinking eyes. His tail fin was wounded. Priscilla understood. The fish couldn't keep up with the rest and he'd be left behind. Once trapped, he'd lose his colours and his plump pink flesh. He's turn a dull black on the outside and no one would want him. He'd be left to die.

Priscilla tried to think of a way to fix his tail fin. Remembering what a doctor had done when she broke a finger. She wrapped the wounded fin in seaweed, placed two sticks around it and wrapped it again. She instructed the fish to stay put in the nearest wave.

When Priscilla returned the next day, the fish felt livelier. With time it was able to swim out of its bandage, though it remained in the little wave until it grew strong enough to make the journey to the sea. Priscilla breathed a sigh of relief when he finally swam away. She knew it would make it to the winter feeding grounds.

Bird Magic

There were only a few days left before Christmas. The song of a bird woke Priscilla out of a deep sleep. She got up and followed the sound to her window and pulling back the curtain, could see only darkness. There was no sign of a bird.

The song was unlike any she had ever heard before. The bird or whatever creature had sung soon made a habit of coming around. It was the third night it happened.

The next morning she decided to make a search of Beach Village. Even if it meant walking the full length of the shore, through the fields or deep into the woods, she'd find it! She spent the day listening and looking. There were no unusual sounds, or for that matter any animals or birds in sight. It was all very discouraging.

That night Priscilla found herself waiting for the song. She felt restless and sleep wouldn't come. She decided to open her window. Maybe whatever it was would enter. The thought of something scary coming through the window made her shiver but she was determined. She sat propped by pillows waiting but nothing happened.

Suddenly the song returned. It was livelier and lovelier than ever. Her eyes opened and there stood a glowing bird. The feathers were a brilliant soft gold with a touch of white at the edges and a fan of delicate ones on its head. The bird sang in a melodious way. Priscilla giggled with delight. The song took on words. Not that birds speak like humans!

But listening carefully, the notes formed words. Priscilla understood.

"I'm a sparkling bird of gold,
I've come to top your Christmas tree,
And set it all aglow".

"Who sent you?" the little girl questioned.

"I'm a gift from a Canadian Goose
I was caught and he set me loose.
I am here to top your tree.
And then I'll be free."

Priscilla laughed. How thoughtful of her goose friend to send such a beautiful gift! She knew the goose was in hiding, as was his custom during special days of the year. When the Simms put up their Christmas tree, the magical bird was placed on top and sometimes it broke into song.

On Christmas Eve everything was very quiet in Beach Village. Priscilla Simms was in bed when she heard chatter followed by a hearty laugh. She crept out of bed and down the stairs. There before the tree was Santa himself. The magical bird was telling Santa how he'd come to be a gift from the Canadian Goose who was in hiding as was his custom over Christmas and New Year's. Priscilla watched Santa's tummy as it shook up and down and around when he laughed. He reached in his big sack and out came a beautiful doll and as if by magic, a toboggan, books and a game.

She watched the old man depart through the grate into the fireplace. He was a short little man, but very round, so round that Priscilla wondered if he'd ever make it up through the chimney to the roof. As if by magic again, she could hear the sounds of Santa and his reindeer as they left for the homes of boys and girls in other places.

Priscilla spent Christmas week playing indoors with the toys that were left beneath her tree. On New Year's Day she decided to try her new toboggan. She opened the door and the magic bird squawked and sang...

"You must now set me free,
For southern warmth I now shall crack
Besides, Canada Goose is back."

Priscilla put out her finger for the magic bird. She took him outside and it flew away. She watched as it disappeared into the distance. Then she searched for a sliding place. It wasn't until she reached the snow-covered beach near the wharf that she found a suitable place. The toboggan had just started down the slope when Canadian Goose glided over and landed before her on the curled up side of the

toboggan. Priscilla couldn't see to steer. She landed on something and whatever it was, it scratched and hurt. It was a piece of driftwood sticking up from the snow. The little girl was very annoyed.

"Look what you made me do," she complained to the goose.

The goose, ashamed, stood with his head hung low. Priscilla, realising that his feelings were hurt, flung her arms around him. He'd given her the best Christmas present of all, the magic bird.

Attack

January was the best month of the winter season in Beach Village on the Miramichi. When Priscilla Simms pulled the blinds up in the morning, a scarlet sun greeted her. The sun was lovelier than at any other time of year. It was a new year and it seemed to bring with it a new sun, fresh but not blinding like the sun of summer. It blazed until it reached its proper height in the sky. Priscilla hurried until she was out in the open. Then she stopped for a long breath of cool fresh air.

"Yonk...Yonk..." she called.

The Canadian Goose, who was hiding and waiting, honked back. He was playing games. His colours were grey, brown and black so when he stood near a bush, he could hardly be seen. Priscilla looked at all the little bushes until she noticed what looked like little black button specks.

"There you are," she said.

The Goose, still in a playful mood, honked again. Then, he crept up and gave her a push from behind. The little girl jumped on his back and they took off. They flew over the village to the forest. Beneath in the woods she could see a herd of deer. As they rode on, she noticed bobcats jumping from tree to tree in search of food. One cat had his eye on a partridge.

"We had better warn it," she whispered.

The Goose honked and the bird heeded and flew away. The bobcat noticed what happened and snarled at Priscilla and the flying goose. Suddenly, other cats joined him until there were about twelve in all. They followed below as the goose flew above.

"Let's turn back," Priscilla begged.

The goose, still in a playful mood, enjoyed the chase and flew further into the woods. He swooped down and then up. Priscilla squealed and scolded. The big bird slowed down and turned. The cats followed on below.

Priscilla sensed that the goose was growing tired. It was no longer a game. If only she had minded her own business and had not warned the partridge, this would never have happened.

Priscilla closed her eyes and did not dare open them again, that is until she felt the goose descend. When her eyes opened, there was only a small clear stretch of snow before they were home. They were safe. Watching the late afternoon sun it seemed almost golden as it set. Somehow it promised an even better tomorrow.

Preparation for a Birthday

Music roared through Priscilla Simms' house in Beach Village on the Miramichi. She was alone and turned the radio on full in hopes of drowning out the frosty noises and the groans of an empty house. Her parents had gone out and the weather, so on and off all winter, had changed again to a real winter's night. Like the music, the weather was in a real lively mood. The wind was at the height of its fury. It blew drifts so high that Priscilla feared her parents wouldn't make it back before morning.

The house took on certain stillness at night. The sounds were weird and frightening, not like the sounds heard during the day. The lights flickered and Priscilla hoped they wouldn't go out. Just to be prepared, she took the candles stored in the bookcase and set them into holders.

The music stopped and was replaced by a man's voice. He spoke about the Centennial. Priscilla wasn't sure what that meant, but the voice went on to explain that it was Canada's birthday in 1967 and that cities, towns and villages were all planning something special. Priscilla had heard of no preparations at Beach Village. There were so few people that it would be almost impossible to collect for a worthwhile project. Priscilla thought there must be something they could do. But it was hard for a little girl to plan such a big thing by herself.

It was, however, better than thinking of scary things. She turned the radio down. The voice had been replaced by music. There wasn't much to see except the snow that covered the veranda. Beyond that, only the darkness of the night could be viewed.

Suddenly, a ghost-like creature appeared. Priscilla ran back and flung herself on the couch. She heard a honk. It was none other than the Canadian Goose. She opened the door and in he came looking very strange with snow piled in a heap over his back.

Priscilla greeted him with a friendly pat. As she did, he spread his wings and the snow fell to the ground. The goose quieted down and the girl sat beside him and repeated the man's story of the birthday. She wondered if he might, along with his flock, get together with the seagulls for an air show over Beach Village at that time. She was sure they could perform even better than the planes.

After all, planes were man-made and only copied birds who were naturals. As if the goose really understood, she went on to say that the machines were taking all the flying glory these days and it was high time that birds showed their skill.

Those were the last words she remembered saying before she awoke to find her head resting on the goose's feathers. It was daylight. The bird became restless and Priscilla opened the door to let him out. Though it had stopped snowing, it was still blustery out. As it was still early, Priscilla fell asleep again and didn't wake up until her parents arrived. With their return, the house became alive again.

Soon a cheerful fire blazed and the odour of food was tantalizing. It was so cosy that she had forgotten the angry storm that had been outside, that is, until a bright light caught her eye through the window. It was the sun. She looked out and all was calm and when she went out, there was warmth in the air. The deep snow prevented her from going anywhere in particular. She just rolled over the snow swells.

Hearing a honk brought her attention to the sky where a flock of geese and seagulls flew in formation over the house. They did all kinds of acrobatics, tricks that even the sky machines had never yet attempted. The Canadian Goose had understood after all. He joined in to wish Canada a Happy Birthday in 1967.

Cooking up a Storm

Sunbeams danced on the snow-covered bay giving a look of glitter to Beach Village on the Miramichi. Everything seemed to sparkle. Priscilla Simms walked out to the open cut in the ice to jiggle her line for smelts. Canadian Goose joined her. His flock would be flying north soon and he was getting anxious, almost as anxious as Priscilla was herself waiting for spring and summer, the seasons that brought playmates of her own size to the village. The goose squatted quietly on the ice next to the little girl. Neither the girl nor the bird made a sound.

The line started to pull and Priscilla jumped to her feet quickly. Something had been hooked. Priscilla pulled but whatever it was couldn't or wouldn't budge. The goose, trying to assist, flapped his wings until Priscilla loosened the line. The bird looked down into the water and made a dive.

The little girl became frantic as she looked into the water and saw the goose and another creature struggling. It seemed to be too big for a fish. They seemed caught up with each other until a little white face appeared above water. It had soft of brown eyes reflecting honesty and sadness. Priscilla loved it on sight. But before she had time to help it up, it had jumped and landed on the ice. It was a little seal.

As it landed, its beautiful coat slipped down exposing slimy flesh. Poor little creature! He had been almost skinned alive by seal hunters. He looked pathetic with his big eyes growing watery as if tears were about to explode. He needed mending. Priscilla fumbled through her clothes until she found a pin. She pulled up his fur coat and put it together until he was restored.

An angry honk brought their attention to the smelt hole. The goose struggled out of the ice water and scolded them in a furious way. Priscilla was just about to be sympathetic when a strong odour reached her nostrils. The smell must have reached the goose as his bill turned up to a sharp point. They were all sniffing upwards into the air. Then, as if the sense of smell was not enough to unravel the mystery, they looked around.

Ahead and behind, they looked. Sideways, they looked. They looked behind again and spotted a little man brewing goodness knows what. Priscilla, followed by the goose and the seal, walked over to investigate the funny little man and his strange brew.

"What are you doing?" she demanded.

"It's obvious. I'm cooking," came the reply.

"What are you cooking?" Priscilla asked.

"I'm brewing up a storm for St. Patrick's day. It's always the last snow storm of the year here," he replied.

"We don't want a storm this year," she protested.

The little leprechaun explained that it had to be and he stirred his terrible brew.

"You're a nasty little creature," Priscilla scolded.

"Could ye tell me if ye are an Irish cailín?" he asked.

"I've some Irish blood on my mother's side," she replied. "Besides, look," she stammered and pulled the little seal over to show how he had been mended.

"This creature is recuperating. Please, we don't really need a storm on the Miramichi this year."

Priscilla, the goose and the seal watched the little man quietly until he laughed. They all laughed, and like the true Irish spirit, the anger dissolved as quickly as it had come. The leprechaun turned his brew over on the ice. It back-fired with a loud bang and went straight up in a narrow line, so high that it touched and turned a white cloud pink.

That was the end of a bad brew and the St. Patrick's storm that year on the Miramichi.

Too much play

Priscilla Simms' father had his salmon nets hung out on racks in the yard in Beach Village. He hauled his white boat down to the shore and launched it in the bay. It was anchored close to the shore.

Priscilla decided to wade out, climb aboard and ride the waves. She took off her shoes and waded into the water in her bare feet. It was icy cold, almost unbearable.

The water was up to her thighs before she reached the boat. She tried climbing in but it was higher than expected. She jumped and reached the edge but couldn't pull herself over. Her fingers slipped and she was in the water again all wet. Her feet felt numb and stiff from the cold and it was an effort walking ashore.

Priscilla sat on the beach, shivering in her wet clothes. She was tired. It was cold and she moved closer to the breakwater out of the wind. Suddenly she saw a huge rock jut out of the water. It moved and splashed! She was fascinated until its head bobbed out of the water. "It must be a whale," she murmured.

She was about to move but before she could, the fish caught sight of her. He was at the edge of the water now, smiling. At least his wide mouth was open in what looked like a smile. Priscilla hoped he was smiling, but then again, it was difficult to tell how fish smiled.

"Please don't eat me, Mr. Whale," she begged.

"I'm not a whale. I'm a porpoise," he replied.

"Well, whatever you are, don't eat me," she begged again.

The porpoise's expression became serious then changed back to being cheerful again. He rolled over and acted silly and playful for a fish. Then he rested again on his tummy, just smiling (or what might be a smile). "You don't look very tasty," he smiled.

"No, I'm not really, not tasty at all," she stuttered.

Just then the most remarkable thing happened. Crabs, oysters, lobsters and fish crept out of the bay to the beach beyond.

"Now look what you've done. You've frightened them," Priscilla scolded.

The porpoise yawned. Priscilla looked very angry. She forgot about her own fear and became very brave.

"You're a nasty fish. You've frightened all the life out of Miramichi Bay".

The little fish, oysters, crabs and lobsters on the beach beyond all applauded loudly. The porpoise looked bored.

"If you don't leave, they'll all die on the shore."

The porpoise laughed. He swam out to the white boat and back. He seemed to want to play.

Priscilla remembered that she had brought her ball with her. It was in her pocket. She took it out and bounced it on a big rock. The porpoise watched. He made a funny noise. Priscilla threw him the ball. The porpoise caught it and flipped it back with his nose. They played catch until the little girl could hardly stand. She decided to stop but the porpoise wanted to play on. He didn't tire of the game.

Finally, the little girl had an idea. She threw the ball to him, said he could keep it but he would have to find a more playful friend, that she was too tired. The porpoise, delighted with the toy, flipped it with his nose, caught it and swam playfully away. The sea creatures applauded once again before returning to the bay and Priscilla ran home.

Collecting Maple Syrup

Early Springtime was "in-between" weather. It was too late to slide and too early to skip. There didn't seem to be anything a little girl or boy could do outdoors.

Priscilla Simms started to plant seeds in one of the flowerpots her mother had given her. At least there would be roots ready for the garden when the frost left the ground. She was just getting the soil ready when she heard voices in the yard. She ran to the window and there was old Mr. Bloom from Back Village standing with his eight grandchildren. Priscilla put up the window and the children called out and asked her to join them in a hunt for maples. They were going to get syrup.

Priscilla called out to her mother, telling her where she was going, but she was so excited that she didn't wait for a reply. She dressed quickly to join the group and was on her way. They walked until they came to the maple 'orchard' as it was named. Mr. Bloom stopped and eyed the trees carefully. Then he hammered what looked like a large nail or spike into a tree, took it out and screwed a little tap in where the nail had been. He did this to ten trees, one for everyone in the group.

The children could not choose their own tree. They had to win their tree. Numbers were placed in a basket on the ground. The children joined hands, forming a circle and danced around. After the song and dance, they went one by one to the basket and picked a number. Priscilla picked number three. Then it occurred to her that she had forgotten to bring a can to catch the running sap. Luckily, Mr. Bloom had brought an extra supply with him, and so he passed a container to her.

Priscilla turned on the tap and while the sap dripped slowly, she joined the others. They were tearing strips of bark off the nearby birch trees. Mr. Bloom made a fire and when the cans were full, the sap was put in a large pot to boil. While the sap cooked, Mr. Bloom made birch bark boxes for everyone. Some of the boiled sap was poured on the snow to harden. Once hard, it was broken into pieces and put into the bark boxes. There were take-home sweets for everyone. Priscilla's cheeks were rosy from her outing. It was dusk and Mrs. Simms was happy to see them. After her dinner Priscilla put a piece of maple taffy in her mouth, feeling that "in-between" weather was fun after all.

Lost in the Woods

As she tramped through the woods, Priscilla Simms wished that she hadn't talked herself into leaving Beach Village at all. The walking was so poor that her feet were buried in slush. It was just that earlier, it had been so sunny outside that it seemed like a good day to do something.

Priscilla hadn't been to the Miramichi woods for a while so she had headed off quickly for the trees. The further Priscilla walked, the deeper the slush became. She was soon up to her knees in wet snow. The wet made her cold and uncomfortable and the trees prevented the sun from shining through.

She was about to turn back when she heard voices. She stood listening, and not being able to make out the conversation, she followed the sound to discover three little girls. They were wet, frightened and lost. One girl had fallen full-length into the slush. Her teeth chattered and her body shivered. Her leg was twisted and she couldn't walk without pain.

Priscilla knew a short cut to her house in Beach Village. One girl stayed with the injured friend and the other followed her to a clearing and then into thick woods again. There they saw a broken down tree house. Boards of grey weathered wood lay on the ground sticking out of the snow. Priscilla brushed snow off an old door and called to the girl to help her drag it back to the others.

Priscilla told the hurt girl to lie on the door and they would all pull her. However, he girl didn't want to and stood shivering.

"Then you'll have to stay here all night," Priscilla warned.

The hurt one looked around at the thick forest and let the girls guide her to the board. It wasn't easy but with scarves tied through holes in the door, the girls were able to pull the door like a sled. Working together, they were soon in Beach Village.

When they reached Priscilla's home, Mrs. Simms made hot cocoa and sat them in front of the fireplace to dry out their clothes. Under their coats, the girls had on Girl Guide uniforms. They had taken a hike in the woods without telling their leader, nor for that matter their families. Mrs. Simms phoned their parents.

After the girls left for home by bus, Priscilla felt lonelier than ever. A few weeks later she was just getting used to being alone again when a group of Guides arrived. They called for Priscilla and took her down to the bay ice. They lit a campfire, played games and sang songs. Priscilla had more fun than she could ever remember!

Somehow, someday, she too would become a Girl Guide.

The Easter Bunny's Secret

The week had been a dull one. The sky was dull. The land and even the bay were as well. Priscilla Simms felt bored. Even the Canadian Goose kept away. Maybe the geese had returned from their flight south and her wildlife friend had joined them. Restless from playing indoors too long, she pulled on her rubber boots and decided to search for some form of life outdoors. The slushy snow made walking unpleasant. She followed footprints in the snow down the lane, not knowing or caring exactly where they led. The fishermen had nets spread out over the rafters and some had already prepared their lobster traps.

Sighting a forestry lookout, Priscilla decided to go there and take a closer look. The further she walked, the further the tower seemed to be. Finally though, she arrived, taking the time to sit rather than look over the tall ladder-like tower. While not looking or watching for anything in particular, she noticed a group of white bunnies approach. They stopped briefly, and then ran quickly away.

This aroused Priscilla's curiosity, so much that before she could even consider, she climbed up the steel structure until she reached a platform to try to catch sight of them. They were nowhere in sight. Probably the bunnies were too tiny to spot from such a high place. She glanced around and was amazed to see down into a clearing in the forest.

Little squirrels were coming out of their winter's hideaway. They yawned, stretched and giggled. Then out of a nearby den lumbered two big bears. They also yawned. The bears and squirrels were still yawning when a herd of deer joined them. From then on it was like one big party, the friendliest time in the animal kingdom, a time before the fight for existence would begin for another year.

She looked over and down towards the village. On the nearest farm and just outside of the fence on a dark patch of land, she noticed the group of white bunnies. The sun broke through. A big rooster approached. He walked with his head held high and was most dignified indeed. It was almost Easter, the one time of the year when hens laid only for bunnies.

Priscilla, anxious to see what would happen next, decided to climb down. This was a much more difficult task than climbing up. Taking very careful steps, she made it to the ground.

Making sure she was very quiet, she walked over to the farm. The rooster strutted back to the hen house and was followed by the tiny anxious rabbits that collected eggs from all the hens. The dignified rooster picked at a bundle of straw in the corner until it uncovered a golden wagon loaded with eggs. Then the magic of the rooster coloured the eggs every colour of the rainbow, even adding sparkles to some of them. With the same magic, he turned some of them into chocolate. The bunnies, wagon and eggs then disappeared.

The farmer arrived and went into the hen house. He counted and shook his head. The dignified rooster crowed. Priscilla Simms went home feeling better. She knew the secret of the Easter Bunny.

New Home for a Sea Creature

The fog lifted. It was the first of May and the weather was so cold that icicles hung down from the roof at Priscilla Simms' home in Beach Village on the Miramichi. Priscilla climbed on the veranda rail, reached up and broke one off. She took a bite and found it tasty enough to go on eating.

The Canadian Goose swooped down and then flew up again. Priscilla didn't pay too much attention to it. She had to check on the little seal that had been left to live at the edge of the bay. He was nowhere in sight when she reached the beach. Priscilla felt panicky. Though the animal slept under the great swells of the bay, he always appeared on shore in the mornings. Priscilla walked up and down calling "Pinup", the name she had given the little seal. The Canadian Goose landed and joined her in the search.

Finally the goose honked and took off. He circled in one particular area. Flying upward, he then made a nose dive down and as he did, Pinup the seal jumped out of a swell and raced onto the shore. The seal clung to the little girl. He shivered and his usually lovable eyes looked frightened. Priscilla had never seen her playful little friend in such a state before. He blurped and pointed out to the bay. His blurpy talk was so mixed up that Priscilla couldn't make out what he was trying to say. The bird joined them on the shore and listened.

"He says there are great sea monster ghosts in the water," the goose explained. Priscilla laughed.

"You've just had bad dreams," Priscilla said trying to comfort the little seal. He shook his head.

Priscilla threw a rubber ball and Pinup bounced it back on his nose in a matter of fact way. He just wasn't his cheerful, happy self and there was no use trying to make him so. Then the goose had a plan to reassure Pinup that the sea monsters were just a part of his dream. He volunteered to make a search of the Bay with his keen eyes. He spread his big wings and took off into the sky over the water.

Pinup and Priscilla watched as the bird skillfully scanned the Bay. Shortly afterwards something was sighted as they could see the goose circle around one area in particular in preparation for his famous dive. He flew up and glided down and as he hit the water, a big sea monster emerged. It was horrid and larger than anything ever imagined to be sea life on the Miramichi.

The monster with what seemed to be one great swoop, reached the shore. Priscilla trembled. The goose honked his loudest honk. Pinup was so weak he could not balance himself and had to lean on the little girl for support. Priscilla opened her mouth to speak but she couldn't.

"I've come to gather and take all little lost seals," the monster announced.

The goose landed in front of Priscilla and Pinup and spread his great wings to hide and protect his friends from the fierce-looking monster. However, the Bay was suddenly full of the creatures and there was no escape.

The Canada goose was no longer brave. He trembled and took refuge beside Priscilla. She felt the fear from her animal friends and somehow this brought out her courage. She shouted:

"You bullies! You Sea monsters! You're not going to take Pinup away. I won't allow it,"

"We're hooded seals. We've come to offer a home, not harm," the big one replied.

Pinup, wriggling himself free, dove through the swells until he reached the monster. The goose honked a warning from the shore. Pinup slid over the big one's back and became his old self again. He sat at the top of a wave and it rolled him back onto the shore. He blurbled a "thank-you" and took off, as he joined the hooded seals of the bay.

Under Water

Beach Village looked and felt beautiful, the way a village should on the first day of summer. Priscilla Simms took a deep breath filling her lungs with fresh air. She had spent the morning untangling nets for her father and decided to wander down to the beach. She felt a bit tired. She sat down and as she did, she noticed a sea sponge. She fingered it and lay back yawning.

The sound of "click, click, click" startled her. She sat up and there was a giant lobster walking towards her on the beach flat stones. The lobster walked slowly. He looked ugly; his colour was greenish black. He lifted a claw and it snapped open and it snapped closed. This frightened Priscilla.

"Why, just one snap and he could slice off a finger," she muttered. She got up and tried to run but her legs wouldn't move. They were frozen with fear. Finally, they got started but it was too late. The lobster had hold of her long hair. She was trapped.

"Please let go," she cried. She tried wriggling away but this only made matters worse. "What do you want?" she asked.

"I want to show you Lobster City," he replied.

Priscilla thought for a moment and decided to do what he asked and told him so in a meek voice. The Lobster let go of her hair and commanded her to climb on his back.

The little girl felt uncomfortable on the lobster's back. He was cold, hard and slippery. When he started walking, Priscilla had to take hold of his two feelers, holding them like reins. They reached the sea and the little girl took a deep breath as she felt herself go down into the water. They went down, down, and down until they reached the floor of the bay. The lobster crept along. Priscilla noted that they were in a desert land, so to speak. This was not for long as they began to pass strange sea farmlands.

Eventually they arrived at the most fascinating place Priscilla had ever seen.

The buildings were made of sponge. The streets were narrow, lined with gardens of green colourful growth and stones. The colours were unlike anything she had seen on the land. The lobster stopped crawling and the little girl hopped off to inspect the mysterious city. Fish swam by, fish that were unfamiliar in colour and shape. They were fish that reflected light. Shells lay near the sponge buildings, shells of all shapes and colours.

They looked as if they'd make good seats. She sat down on one. That was a mistake because suddenly she was popping up and she was popping down. She looked down and an angry head popped out. It was alive.

Back on her own two feet again, she noticed that the lobster had disappeared.

"He has to be found", she thought, "or I will never find my way home again."

She called but instead of sound, bubbles sprang from her mouth. She walked through the narrow streets brushing against the buildings as she went. She arrived at a wide street and suddenly, hundreds of lobsters appeared from behind the sponge house. They seemed friendly.

Priscilla stood quietly waiting for something to happen. The lobsters turned and bowed.

"You are to be our Queen," the biggest lobster announced.

Priscilla objected and tried to talk but only bubbles came out. The lobsters marched her over to a large sponge house. She entered. It was furnished in shiny stones. Water sprouted in and water sprouted out. It was extraordinary.

"It's lovely but I can't stay," she tried to say. Only bubbles came out. The lobsters' claws opened and closed in protest as if they had understood. Priscilla then realised, with concern, that she could not get out of her sponge house.

Suddenly, the lights went out in the fish city and Priscilla felt alone and trapped. She heard a sharp noise and when she awoke, she found herself on the beach, clutching a sponge in her hand.

Baby Birds

On the Miramichi in June, the evenings are like daylight. Darkness doesn't fall until some time after children's bedtime. Priscilla Simms of Beach Village hated going to bed then. She couldn't sleep until Nature drew its blinds across the sky.

One evening she looked out only to see the big tree near her house covered with an army of blackbirds. The sight of the beautiful tree became rather ugly. There was something weird and frightening about the birds being there.

Priscilla felt sure that something important was going on in the bird world. She thought that maybe the blackbirds had declared war on the little birds. She watched and suddenly the birds grew restless. They scolded and flew around every way, not like birds usually do at all. Priscilla knew they were excited about something.

"But about what?" she wondered.

There were no other birds in the surrounding trees. In fact, there were no other birds in sight. She leaned further out of the window and as she did she noticed a long-haired cat, and on the ground, barely visible was a wee bird, either maimed or too young to fly. The blackbirds swooped down on the animal but the cat marched on. Priscilla ran down the stairs, grabbed a mop and chased the cat from the yard. Sure enough, a young blackbird struggled on the grass.

Priscilla tried to pick him up but she couldn't get hold of him at all. She didn't want to get bitten so she ran back into the house and put her mother's gardening gloves on. They were so big that they would be awkward for picking up anything, let alone a wee bird.

When she tried, the bird snapped at the empty fingers of the gloves. She was timid and couldn't get a firm grip. The little bird spread his wings and hopped ever so quickly into the bush. Priscilla followed, and with courage, grabbed the bird quickly and placed him in the crevice of the big tree. She returned to the house and the window.

There was not a blackbird in sight.

Priscilla wondered why they were not around to help, but then she looked up and noticed the wee bird climb higher into the trees. She held her breath, thinking he might fall again.

Then another bird, probably the mother, flew cautiously behind from branch to branch until it reached the baby and Priscilla knew all was well.

Little Warrior

The trees were beginning to dress for summer in Beach Village. Priscilla Simms decided to go to the woods and watch the buds on the branches burst into their leaves. She was very excited at the thought of the fresh, new, green leaves. She planned to spend the day just watching but after an hour or so she decided that the buds were not yet ready. Maybe they wouldn't come out at all if they felt they were being watched.

She left and started collecting pine twigs for the pretty jug she had found on the beach last summer. She pulled back a branch and there was a small animal looking at her in the face. He wasn't very pretty as he had a rather small, sharp face framed by brownish and whitish hair that stood up on end. It was a porcupine.

Priscilla didn't dare move as she thought maybe the porcupine might start shooting his quills. She stayed quiet. Finally, the porcupine scampered off to feed on another tree. Priscilla watched him. He didn't look like a very lovable animal and he certainly didn't look cuddly.

Priscilla decided it would be safer if she took off. She started to walk but still being interested in budding trees, she didn't watch where she was going and tripped over a fallen branch. She couldn't get up and thought her leg must be broken. She lay on the ground for quite a while and all the time she laid there, the porcupine kept watching as he chewed on a pine tree trunk.

Priscilla was happy when she heard a little dog bark. He appeared and went right over to sniff at Priscilla. He was very friendly. The porcupine thought the little dog was going to hurt her and ran out, shooting his quills as he did so. The poor little dog squealed. He was full of porcupine needles! He ran away and Priscilla could hear his squeals for some time. In the meantime, the warrior moved closer to Priscilla, sat down and shot everything in sight.

Priscilla was beginning to feel uncomfortable. Her legs were hurting and she was worried how she would be rescued. The warrior just wouldn't allow anyone to come close enough to pick her up. She scolded but he only looked at her. His face was almost cute and kind of funny. Priscilla laughed.

She reached out to stroke his back. It was lovely and soft and not sharp at all.

But suddenly, he became needle-like again! The little dog, along with a group of people, had arrived. The warrior shot his small spears every way. The people scattered and hid behind the trees and the dog did likewise. He didn't want to get shot again!

Priscilla reached out and stroked the little warrior's needles. She calmed the animal down and as soon as he was nice and fluffy again, she grabbed him and held him tight. She thanked him for guarding her and said goodbye, and then he scampered off further into the woods.

The people came out of hiding and went over to Priscilla. She was glad to have met the porqupine, but even more glad when one of the men picked her up and carried her home.

Marie Therese of Acadian Village

Entangled

"Maman, we got a post card. It has a picture of an alligator on it" cried Marie Therese excitedly. "Who's it from?"

Her mother smiled when she turned over the card.

"It's from Aunt Sophie. You know. You met her last year at the family reunion. She says she is coming again this summer."

"How come she lives in a faraway place and is still family?"

Marie Therese looked out through frosted windows at coloured leaves blown about the yard by cold Autumn winds and shivered. It would be nice to lie in the heat like an alligator.

"Aunt Sophie's ancestors had to move away a long time ago.

It was a time of kings and wars and new lands. Aunt Sophie may live in a swamp in Louisiana, but she is still Acadian as you and me."

A puppy with charcoal shaggy fur and big brown eyes scratched at the door wanting attention.

"I think it's time to give the dog a name, Maman."

"Ah non, ma petite. Don't get too attached to that dog. It must belong to someone in town and they will come looking for him one day."

The orphan puppy dog had followed Marie Therese everywhere for the past week. Marie Therese loved the little dog. He seemed to want to belong to her. She felt that no one would ever come and that the orphan puppy would always remain with her.

She looked outside. The puppy's tongue was hanging out and he looked like he was smiling. She felt very proud of the little puppy. Being with him made her feel brave enough to go anywhere.

Marie Therese went out to the dog and they started walking in no particular direction through the fields. The new frost had brought about a change and as they approached the dense woods, she sensed that the birds were more restless than usual. The crispness in the air brought on urgent preparations for their trip south.

In the woods she caught sight of squirrels that seemed too busy even to be timid. They were rushing back and forth in search of nuts to store for winter use. Marie Theresa told them to relax. After all, it was just the first nip of frost and shouldn't send them into such a frenzy.

The young dog chased a couple of squirrels, not far though, as they just stopped and stood on their hind legs and faced him. The dog walked away after deciding that the squirrels were not interested in play.

Maria Therese walked out of the woods and back to the field. There were spider tents scattered everywhere over the ground. The webs were made noticeable by beads of dew glittering on the delicate threads. Even the bushes nearby were covered. They were beautiful, unlike the dirtier cobwebs that formed sometimes in her home.

"Spiders were certainly busy workers," she thought. A little shiver went through her as another thought finally came to her. Spiders terrified her. She reached out her hand and slapped the branches free of the webs that bound them.

The little dog barked. Marie Therese turned and, there he was, bound up in a huge web. He tried wiggling out but it was no use. He couldn't even seem to open his mouth to let out another bark. The little girl started over to rescue him when suddenly a huge spider walked straight up a thread and dangled over her head. She stood frozen with shock and before she could move, she was bound like the bushes and the little dog in the spider's web. Though she couldn't move, at least she could see. It was a rather comfortable feeling as the threads were soft. At the same time, they were very tough and she could not break free.

All kinds of dreadful looking insects lit upon her as she stood. It was frightening and she was relieved when she discovered that they couldn't reach her nor could they set them selves free. They were trapped.

An army of brightly coloured spiders appeared. The little girl hadn't realized that spiders could be beautiful. They picked off the threads that bound her and set her free.

They used the strands of web to recover the bushes, and as they worked, they paid no attention to the little girl whatsoever. They danced up and down in a slow rhythm. Marie Therese realized how warm and safe the bushes really were under the web. "I've changed my mind about spiders. You only protect Nature," she thought.

Suddenly she remembered the dog. He was still caught. "Would you free my dog?" she asked the spiders. They did so, and it was like watching a special performance. They withdrew one thread at a time. Once the dog was free, he barked and ran about to spend his energy.

"Silly dog," she said. "You are nothing but trouble". The dog looked up at her as if it understood.

"Wait a minute. That's what I'll call you. Come on 'Troubles'."

The little dog trotted happily behind. Marie Therese returned home, happy with the knowledge that Troubles had a names and that spiders were Nature's friends.

For Keeps

It was smelt fishing time in the village, and Marie Therese's daddy was down on the bay ice straightening his nets. The litlle girl decided to walk out to the ice village, where there were little tiny huts lined up along the shore. Fishermen moved in from other places to fish for the small silver smelts by setting nets through the ice. Marie Therese knew they must be warm, because smoke came out of the chimneys.

Troubles, the orphan puppy, was very nosey and before Marie Therese could warn him, the dog entered a hut and headed straight for some biscuits left on the table in the shabby little room. Before she could stop the dog, it had gobbled every one of them.

"You're a bad puppy dog. I gave you a good name," Marie Therese said.

The puppy followed her out to the nets. It all looked strange to Marie Therese. There were two poles standing up with a narrow bar across. On the ground, Marie Therese noticed a hole in the ice, and looking even closer, she saw the water.

"That's where the nets are, Troubles," she told the dog. There was no sign of her daddy, and there were no fishermen around because there was no work to do until it was time to pull up the nets again.

Marie Therese and Troubles ran back to shore. The cold made Marie Therese's cheeks as rosy as apples. The sun was setting and it was time to go home. When she reached the house, Troubles squealed.

"What's wrong?" she asked.

The puppy lifted his paws. Ice was caked solidly between his toes. So Marie Therese picked him up and brought him into the house. Marie Therese's mother scolded but when she found out how cold the puppy was, she let him stay in.

Once in the door, the dog made itself at home. Marie Therese turned out to be right. No one ever came to claim Troubles, and he became her very own puppy dog.

Too Excited

There were miles of snow ahead. Marie Therese followed her Daddy and the fishermen on snowshoes. Troubles ran ahead and then behind. He ran ahead to see that all was clear, and behind to see that the little girl was still with them. Marie Therese felt tired. She couldn't tell the men how miserable she felt. They had not wanted her to come for just that very reason. They were going out on the frozen Miramichi Bay to check their nets.

It was a clear day. A group of tree tops marked the islands from a distance. The snowshoes felt heavy on the little girl's feet and she stopped. 'Troubles' ran back. He jumped, putting his two front paws on the little girl's legs. Marie Therese brushed the dog's feet off. She turned back to the Village. 'Troubles' stood and watched.

"Come. Allez vite", Marie Therese called.

Troubles ran to the little girl. His tail wagged and his tongue hung out at the side of his mouth. They reached the village road. Marie Therese took off her snowshoes and carried them to the fish shed.

When Marie Therese opened the door, birds came from all directions, from under and over the wooden beams. They flew every way.

Troubles barked. He ran around making the birds excited.

"Stop Troubles, you'll scare the birds," Marie Therese scolded.

Troubles was having too much fun to stop. The dog chased itself and barked as the birds flew nervously out of reach. The little dog didn't listen. It loved to play, and this was play to it.

Suddenly one little bird got so excited, he hit a beam and fell down to the shed floor. "Troubles', still thinking it was play, went over and nudged the bird with his nose, and then stood back and barked.

"Look what you have done, you naughty thing."

The poor little bird," Marie Therese said as she examined it.

One wing was torn and bleeding. She wrapped it in a hanky and ran to the village store. Tears filled her big brown eyes as she showed the little bird to the storekeeper.

He took the bird and examined it carefully. Then he got some alcohol, adhesive and gauze from the shelf and bandaged the bird's wounds. It still couldn't walk and it couldn't fly.

When she arrived home, Marie Therese spent all her time nursing the wounded bird. Months passed and the bird grew strong. It was now able to limp and even fly a little. 'Troubles' played gentler games and they became great friends.

Dreams of South

Everyone helped haul spruce trees to a field where they would be piled up by truckers for shipment to other places. Most of the children in Acadian Village were working. There were only a few days left to get them ready so that the trees would arrive in far away places in time for Christmas.

Marie Therese saw a particularly nice tree and placed it carefully on the top of a pile.

"I hope that one goes to Aunt Sophie in Louisiana," she said to herself with fingers crossed.

Troubles enjoyed the trek through the woods, although he was much more of a nuisance than a help. He acted as if he were in charge of the whole operation. The little girl's enthusiasm tickled him.

The girl ran over to a bundle of trees the dog was sniffing and barking at. Marie Therese shouted but Troubles was persistent. She didn't want to try to move the bundle of trees on her own but finally she took a hold of them and rolled them onto the canvas pull. She was exhausted. Troubles was still barking.

"I'm not moving," the little girl said but the dog barked again.

Marie Therese looked closer and discovered a saucy squirrel that even the barking failed to budge.

"Squirrels are supposed to be busy this time of the year," Marie Therese scolded.

"I'm not collecting nuts anymore. I'm riding south with your bundle of trees," he answered.

Marie Therese explained that he'd need food for the journey. The squirrel laughed in reply. Oh, he'd get plenty. There would be no hibernating for him this winter. He was southbound.

Troubles quieted down. Squirrels usually gave him a merry chase.

There was the sound of children approaching. The squirrel landed in one big leap on the canvas pull and hid under the spruce branches before the bundle was hauled away.

Marie Therese went back now and then to see if the bundle had gone, but it stood for two days in the yard. The truckers loaded other bundles and Marie Therese wondered when they would be back to pick up hers. The little squirrel, still hiding among the branches, looked weak from hunger.

Marie Therese tried persuading him to go back to his family. Tears filled the little animal's eyes. He couldn't. It was too late. He hadn't done his share of the work.

Just then she remembered that she still had a bag of peanuts left over from Halloween. She offered it to the squirrel. He decided to take them and return home. They were the tastiest nuts he had ever eaten even though he felt ashamed. He could never tell his family he'd taken off the work season in preparation to head south.

The wee squirrel smiled, like squirrels smile that is, and Marie Therese gave him a kiss on his cold little nose and Troubles gave him a friendly lick. Then the little squirrel scampered off into the woods and they headed home.

The False Thaw

The snow melted and became rather slushy in Acadian Village on the Miramichi. Marie Therese tried tobogganing but found the snow crusty on the mound near her home. It was slushy in the field. Her feet sank every time she took a step, and it was no fun. The weather was warm, more like Spring weather than Winter. The sun tried its best to peek out through the clouds, but somehow it didn't seem to make it.

Marie Therese and her dog Troubles made for the shore road to the wharf. Bare tarmac, free of ice and snow, felt good underfoot. The river looked unchanged though. Marie Therese expected to see open water. Her Mother said this was a January thaw so she thought everything would melt. Her snowman in the backyard had melted. All that remained of him was a lump of snow.

There was nothing to do on the shore, nothing to do on the wharf. The snow that covered the bay still remained a fresh beautiful white. What was left of the snow in the village was a dirty grey. Seagulls glided gracefully around as if expecting the thaw to open enough water for them to dive for fish. Seagulls didn't often come inland during the winter.

The little girl stood watching while Troubles chased and barked at the birds flying above. One seagull broke away from the flock and flew over, landing on the rock nearest Marie Therese. Noticing the bird, she reached out her arm, expecting it to fly away. It spread its wings showing layers of exquisite white feathers.

"We came inland to fish," the seagull said. "We followed the breezes to you."

"I can't feed you all. I'm just a little girl," Marie Therese replied.

The seagull folded his wings. "My flock needs food."

At that moment Troubles ran back to the girl. Taking no notice of the seagull, it then went back to chasing the flock.

"That must be our food," the seagull announced. Its wings spread out while it watched the little dog running out to the snow-covered bay.

"No ... that's my dog!" Marie Therese replied.

The little girl added that she didn't think that Troubles would taste like fish. In fact, she was sure it wouldn't taste good at all.

All at once she remembered seeing a wooden box of salt Tommy cod as she walked along the breakwater on the upper beach.

"I have your feed," she cried happily as she ran to where the box was.

The seagull followed, and after looking the fish over, said: "You kept the promise of the warm winds". And with that, it let out a cry that brought all the seagulls to shore.

Troubles lost courage when he saw the birds all together. It walked meekly over to Marie Therese for protection. She picked it up and walked away wondering if seagulls got thirsty.

The seagulls waited until she reached the road before flying up, diving down again and then up and away into the distance. It seemed that winter was ready to return, gently bringing clean fresh snow to the Miramichi.

Visitors in the House

Mice crept into Marie Therese's house. The little mice went into hiding but Marie Therese's mother caught sight of one and heard others. She set traps, determined to catch them. In the morning when she inspected the traps, they had been set off, the cheese was taken but the mice were gone.

"They must be very clever mice," she said.

Marie Therese was very interested and very curious about the little creatures. She went to bed early but couldn't sleep. She missed her dog Troubles. It usually slept in a basket next to her bed, but lately it preferred to sleep on a cushion on the kitchen floor. Perhaps it was trying to help her mother catch the mice.

The house was silent. Marie Therese's family was asleep. She decided to go downstairs and visit Troubles. Perhaps it would follow her back to her room. She crept out of bed. It was dark and spooky walking through the house at night. She had to feel her way along the hall and down the stairway to the kitchen. The moon shone through the window and gave light. All of a sudden she heard one mousetrap after another snap. She felt along the wall and turned the light on. There was Troubles with a stick between its teeth. It had upset the traps. It was helping the little mice!

Marie Therese was shocked. The dog did not even look ashamed. In fact, it looked very pleased with itself indeed. She was about to scold it when a little mouse appeared and approached the cheese in the sprung trap. It was just about to take a bite when it noticed the little girl. It didn't run into hiding. It just gave a curious stare. Marie Therese decided that it was cute but saucy for a little mouse. It must have decided that Marie Therese wasn't dangerous because it stayed eating the cheese instead of scurrying away.

Soon other little mice joined it. After the meal, Troubles played hide-and-seek with its little friends. They were very tricky and could hide almost anywhere. Troubles lost the game. He curled up on his cushion again and the little mice cuddled up next to him. They were all soon asleep.

Marie Therese didn't know what to do. She knew her mother wanted to get rid of the creatures before they got into the food. They were so adorable, however, that she thought they should go free. It had to be soon because her mother was planning to borrow the neighbour's tomcat the next day and the tomcat would gobble them all up. Marie Therese had to think.

It was very hard to think in the middle of the night. There would be a thought but it would quickly vanish out into the darkness. But a thought did come eventually and it seemed like the right thought.

She crept softly over to the cupboard and took out her minnow net. She scooped up the little mice into the net. She went outside to the barn and placed them gently in the hay. Troubles scratched the door after them. Marie Therese wondered if it would understand. After all they were its little friends.

She turned out the kitchen light and crept upstairs to her room. The little dog followed. It jumped in his basket and, as if nothing had ever happened, he curled up and went to sleep.

Beware the Needles

The Miramichi forest near Acadian Village still had snow blanketing the ground. The little roadway through the woods was muddy, wet and full of ruts. Marie Therese didn't care as she was wearing a new pair of new high rubber boots that kept her feet protected. Her little dog, Troubles, ran ahead. Its feet were very dirty but it was so happy to be out on the trail that it didn't seem to notice.

It saw a rabbit that had not yet turned brown. It stopped, put his nose the air and sniffed. Then Troubles chased the rabbit. Marie Therese scolded it. The poor little rabbit could really be in danger this time of year; it stood out so clearly against the ground. Whether brown or white, in the early Spring a rabbit was completely visible against ground that was neither colour.

The rabbit ran with great speed and Troubles couldn't keep up with him. It disappeared, probably by escaping into the snowy part of the woods. Troubles sniffed into the air and at the trees. Though it sniffed eagerly, it couldn't pick up the scent of the rabbit.

The rabbit was feeling very clever. It ran out, showing himself again to the little dog. Troubles went wild! It barked and chased the rabbit along the trail. It almost caught the end of its fluffy little tail when the rabbit took a hop sideways and disappeared again. It was no longer a game. Troubles was getting really annoyed by being tricked.

As they walked, Marie Therese noticed a piece of snow move along with them. It was the rabbit ready to tease the little dog again! The girl broke off a twig from a nearby tree and threw it, frightening the creature away.

The rabbit ran into a group of spruce trees. Marie Therese entered the woods. If the snow was not too deep, she would collect the gum that formed on their trunks. She had brought along her collecting bag as there was always something to bring home from the woods.

She walked on the hard crust without sinking. She chopped and picked at the sticky gum with her thumb and ended up with a good supply of spruce gum. She put all but one piece in her bag. That one she put in her mouth. At first, it was difficult to chew. It seemed to be falling apart. She continued to chew until it became real gum. How pleased her mother would be! Her mother said spruce gum exercised and strengthened the jaw and was good for the teeth.

Troubles had disappeared. Marie Therese followed its bark to find the dog stopped and staring at some of the strangest little animals she had ever seen! Trouble's tail wagged proudly at having discovered something of its own.

It wasn't long before Marie Therese found out what the creatures were, because soon a large mama porcupine appeared to protect her babies! The girl tried to warn her dog, but it was far too busy wagging his tail and poking the little things in a friendly way. Thinking that Troubles might hurt her little ones, the porcupine attacked.

Poor Troubles! He was full of quills and howled with pain. He wouldn't allow Marie Therese to touch him, and ran all the way home crying, the way dogs cry.

Marie Therese's daddy knew what had happened when they returned home. He took out his pliers and pulled the quills out, one by one. After the operation was over, Marie Therese bathed the dog and wrapped it carefully in a blanket. As it went off to sleep, Marie Therese watched as its feet moved in a little dance. Perhaps it was still chasing the rabbit. Or maybe it was listening to her warning and was running away. Whatever adventures it was now having were in its dreams.

A Secret Place

The ice had completely disappeared. Though the sun was warm, the air was cool. As always after the ice opened each season, it took at least three weeks for the village to warm up. The pussy willows had been out for some time. Marie Therese decided to go picking flowers where she could find shelter from the wind. Usually there were plenty of spots near the hidden river. It was a place not often visited and Marie Therese never ceased to be amazed that she could find it.

She collected a big bunch of willows and stroked the soft pussy-like buds against her cheek. She walked on and before she realized it, she was standing facing the little river. It looked so alive. It seemed happy to be free of the heavy blanket of ice that covered it during the winter. It flowed so quickly over the rocks on its bed that it splashed sprays of water that rose and danced in the air.

Trout jumped around in the water. They seemed to jump to see which one could jump the highest. Marie Therese laughed. There was one that not only jumped the highest but could do a somersault in mid-air.

It was delightful! Soon she discovered that not all the fish were jumping. On the bank she noticed several salmon lying motionless. They had been caught and left by anglers. She put aside the pussy willows and ran over to where they were. Five or six salmon were still breathing. Their gills opened and closed with a heavy beat-like motion and their eyes blinked. They had been caught and left to die.

The little girl ran to a tree and pulled off a branch. She placed the fish on it and floated it along the water, making sure she had a firm grip on the bough. She held on hoping they would wiggle back to life. Watching them, she realized that they were black salmon, fish trapped in the river by the ice when winter arrived early last year.

Marie Therese's arm ached, not from the weight of the branch, but from the fact that her arm was held outstretched. She let go and the jerky movement upset the sick fish. They were gone. Marie Therese sighed. Looking in the water she thought that even if they remained lifeless, they were at home somewhere in the little hidden river, a place they belonged.

In Trouble Again

The fishing boats set sail in Acadian Village early in the morning. All the villagers watched as the boats, loaded with lobster traps, glided out and into the distance on Miramichi Bay. Marie Therese felt very happy as there would be a feed of lobster in her home that night. She wondered what she would do until the boats arrived back at sunset.

She walked around the wharf with her dog Troubles lagging behind. There was something especially good about seeing traps, markers and buoys piled high on the dock. It was good to hear the boats squeak as the choppy little waves rocked them in and out, stretching and loosening the rope as they did so.

Marie Therese climbed down the ladder and boarded one of the boats. Troubles barked. It was too high. It couldn't jump. It made such a noise barking that Marie Therese climbed back up and walked home. She played on the swings in the backyard. It was a long day for Marie Therese.

She spent most of the day wondering about the time. She watched the sun. It seemed forever before it changed its position, and the day took on a new colour. At last it was time to go back to the dock and wait.

The boats arrived with a good lobster catch. The men chatted and laughed with delight. Marie Therese went down the ladder and boarded her father's boat. There were hundreds of lobsters. They were not pretty as they crawled slowly over each other in the pit of the boat.

Left on the dock, Troubles ran back and forth, barking and wagging its tail. It wanted to join Marie Therese but she was too busy to pay any attention to it. Its cries turned to howls, attracting the attention of a fisherman who tried to reach for it. The little dog backed away and took a leap. The fisherman caught him but then fell back himself and Troubles, caught off balance, fell into the pit with the lobsters. Poor little Troubles!

He was so bewildered. Every time he moved, some part of him was snapped at by the many claws around and beneath him. Marie Therese stretched out her hand but she couldn't stretch far enough to reach. Finally, her father jumped into the pit, picked the dog up and handed him to Marie Therese.

The little girl cuddled and sympathized until its cries faded to a quiet moan. The fisherman sold their catch. Troubles, on his feet again, looked into the bucket of lobsters Marie Therese carried. He looked, but he was very careful not to go close enough – even for a good sniff!

Treasure From Long Ago

The fishermen were out in the bay checking on their lobster catch off the Acadian Village. Marie Therese stood watching and praying from the shore bank that the traps would be loaded. Fishing had been slow lately. Marie Therese's father had been so discouraged that he hardly spoke now and he was usually a very talkative man. There was no use waiting for the boats to return. The wait would be too long. The little girl walked back home.

She arrived to hear Troubles' excited barking from the barn. She decided it must have spotted a mouse. She ran over and sure enough, the little dog was running into the hay searching for something. When it wiggled out and discovered Marie Therese, the dog barked and then continued with his search, Marie Therese wandered around the old barn. She climbed up into the loft where she found hay and lamps, books and picture frames discarded by her mother. She examined an old Aladdin Lamp. The lamp had belonged to her Grandpapa. They were used before electricity came into Acadian Village.

Marie Therese carried the Aladdin lamp down the loft ladder. It was a difficult climb down and she was relieved to reach ground level with the lamp still in one piece. She ignored Troubles and ran to show her discovery to Ma Mere, her mother. Marie Therese could have the lamp. She then set about carefully washing it down and polishing it up until its silver gleamed. It was beautiful. Ma Mere filled it with oil and when night fell, she would be permitted to light it.

She ran down to the water. The fishermen had returned and Marie Therese could tell by the happy expressions on their faces that their traps had yielded a rich catch of lobster.

Her father's good humour had returned. The evening was filled with chatter and laughter. When the curtains of night crossed and met in the sky above, Marie Therese lit her Aladdin lamp. It gave off a bright glow, as bright as any of the electric light bulbs used but much softer and prettier.

Though she knew the value of electricity, it was exciting to bring something from the past into the present.

The Boat Festival

People in Acadian Village were busy preparing for the blessing of the fleet. It was a big day for the villagers. Marie Therese could hardly wait to put on her pretty new cotton dress. Her mother had made it out of a fine print.

Relatives arrived from the city for the occasion; an aunt, uncle and a little boy cousin. The boy's name was Pierre. He was full of energy. In fact, he was so full of energy that he tired out Marie Therese. She had never got tired of playing before. Perhaps it was the way Pierre played. He touched all the delicate ornaments in the house, making the grown-ups nervous. He boasted of being able to climb through a crack in the window pane. It was so ridiculous the little girl didn't bother to argue with him.

Troubles hid when Pierre was around. It was no wonder because the boy pulled the dog's tail and yanked at its fur. He poked his eyes and squeezed his neck. Poor Troubles just stayed out of the way now. It hid under the big chair watching the active child sadly, not knowing what to expect next.

Marie Therese found Pierre lovable in many ways. He had a way of smiling that made people forgive him anything. He had a cute way of saying things. It was his curiosity, she decided, that made him the way he was. It could be that little boys learned that way.

Marie Therese felt pretty in her new dress when the day finally came and she was allowed to wear it. Down at the docks, grownups wandered close to the platform to hear speeches while she stayed behind on the side of the dock road with Pierre. They were too little to see above the crowd so they climbed on one of the vessels. Once aboard, they were helped up to the top of the cabin roof.

All the boats were decorated with gay triangle flags and paper flowers. The boats were clean. The scum and scales of fish had been scrubbed from their decks.

Marie Therese was so busy looking that she didn't notice Pierre slip away. He was such a quick little boy that she just looked away for a minute and he was gone. She panicked and jumped down to the deck and walked the plank to the wharf. Pierre was nowhere in sight. She looked over the edge and there he was halfway down the ladder to the sea.

Marie Therese reached down but she couldn't get a grip on his arms. The little boy started crying. A man, hearing the cries, looked over, pushed the little girl aside and brought Pierre safely up. He was quiet for the first time since his arrival in the village and actually looked exhausted. They waited for their parents and when they arrived the little boy was taken home and put to bed.

Marie Therese, able to relax again, looked down at her new dress. It was covered in tar. She cried bitterly, but her mother said that the stain would come out, and took her hand in hers.

Ma Mere led Marie Therese to the shore where cut bullrushes were piled. Taking one in each hand, they dipped them in oil and lit them from the flames of a bonfire. The whole shoreline became alight with torches. People formed a line for miles.

Marie Therese forgot about her stained dress and joined in on the songs and laughter of the crowd.

Pierre the Hero

One day, Pierre, Marie Therese and Troubles the dog, had been playing at the construction yard in Acadian Village. It was a place where little people and dogs had no business being. But the big working machinery made them curious, made them forget the danger of taking a closer look.

Then suddenly, Troubles got in the way of a big crane, which lifted up a pile of rubble, and the dog along with it. It emptied all the rubble into a truck. Everything dropped out except for Troubles. It was caught hanging between the teeth on the mouth of the crane. Pierre climbed the big machine to warn the operator not to bite for more rubble. He made it to the operator just in time to save the dog's life.

Marie Therese left Troubles snugly wrapped in a blanket on the kitchen floor. She was so grateful to Pierre that she would see that he received a special gift for his heroic deed. She headed down the shore road in Acadian Village. When she spotted Simon Savoie, she quickened her pace. Simon was the village chiseler or wood carver and he was out sketching seagulls on the snow-covered beach. She walked quietly so as not to disturb the flock that flew nearby.

Finally she reached him and saw that he was now carving wood. He showed no sign of noticing her presence. He just carved away, the wood chips falling on his clothes and on the ground. He only took time out to spit the juice of his tobacco. He chewed almost continuously.

Marie Therese finally found the courage to disturb him by a pat on the shoulder. She told the carver of the rescue in the construction yard, saying how brave Pierre was and that he deserved a special present. She said that as Simon's birds were the most special carvings of their kind, she wondered if they could make a trade. She unfolded her kerchief showing a collection of birds' eggs.

The wood carver made no comment. His face showed no sign of interest. Marie Therese was trying to think of something else she could swap when the old man placed a completed wooden gull in her hand. It was so lifelike that she could imagine it taking off into flight. She held it firmly in her fist and headed back to the village. But first she turned around and waved to the wood carver.

Reunion

Every year since Marie Therese could remember, and that wasn't long as the old ones kept reminding her, there had been a big family reunion. Acadians had large families but Marie Therese thought hers must be the largest family ever. There was no place big enough to hold the dinner for everyone so they had to put up an enormous tent.

It seemed that Ma Mere and the other women in the village had been cooking forever. Actually, they had started over a month before, baking meat pies, buns and sweet squares. The kitchen was filled with comforting smells. Marie Therese tried to help but she just ended up covered in flour and dropping things. She thought she was doing well until her mother shoo-shooed her from the kitchen. Troubles probably had something to do with it. He had jumped up on her when she was pouring flour. She missed; the flour went everywhere and Troubles went pattering off, leaving little white tracks all over the house.

When all the goodies were ready and cooled, they were packaged up and frozen. The huge freezers were also filled with all kinds of fish and shellfish. Plastic containers held icy blueberries, strawberries and raspberries.

Many people were coming from a long way away, from a place called Louisiana. It was in the United States. They all had the same last name except some of them sometimes pronounced it in an English way. Marie Therese always enjoyed meeting her American family. They were so exotic. They called themselves "Cajuns", instead of Acadians and spoke French in a slow way that made you think of heat, alligators and naps in beds with mosquito netting. Ma Mere said that these Americans used to live here but moved south many many years ago. They didn't look that old! Marie Therese liked to look at their big cars and mobile homes. Their music was lively.

Tonight was the last night of the reunion. Marie Therese always liked this night. Children were allowed to stay up late. It was the night of the big dance.

P'tit Bertrand got out his fiddle, Jean-Claude was on the accordion, Norbert on the piano and Louis on guitar. One old man played the spoons. Another got up to do a step-dance. Mademoiselle Mae got up and sang a slow song.

Marie Therese was sitting beside a woman from Louisiana that she had met the previous year. She called her Tante Sophie. The two had taken to each other at once. Sophie fascinated Marie Therese with tales of the swamp while, in return, she seemed genuinely interested in her account of ordinary life in the village.

"Will you write to me?" asked Tante Sophie.

"Yes of course." Marie Therese put her arms around the large woman and hugged her. When she pulled away, she noticed a tear slowly dropping down the cheek of Aunt Sophie.

"You are a lucky little girl to live in this place, cherie. We never wanted to leave, you know. We had to go."

Marie Therese had always thought that life in Acadian Village was a bit difficult. The winters could be cruel, no one was rich and they had to work hard. She looked around and saw her mother and father smiling at each other as they danced. Outside, a million stars broke out on a black sky. She could faintly hear the sound of water lapping on the shore and a breeze rustling through the trees. She thought she could understand what it would mean to lose this. Even for a big car and alligators.

"Yes, I guess it is a special place," she thought. The dog, Troubles, jealous of the attention she was giving to Sophie, jumped up. She gave him a hug and another to Aunt Sophie, happy to be together with them at that particular time and at place.

Song: The Wink of the Sun

by Nonie Creaghan and Dan Leeman

About Nonie Creaghan

Nonie Creaghan was born on the Miramichi in New Brunswick in 1926. She studied journalism at Columbia University in New York, and was a protégée of Lord Beaverbrook, at The Daily Gleaner in Fredericton before working in radio, television, advertising and other print media.

www.ingramcontent.com/pod-product-compliance
Lightning Source LLC
Chambersburg PA
CBHW041158100726
47911CB00016B/781